SUMMER
ON EARTH

Peter Thompson

1

ISBN: 978-1-943978-30-4

Printed in China

CPSIA Tracking Label Information:
Production Location: Guangdong, China
Production Date: 4/15/2017
Cohort: Batch 68374

Library of Congress Cataloging-
in-Publication Data available.

10 9 8 7 6 5 4 3 2 1

Published by

Persnickety Press
120A North Salem Street
Apex, NC 27502

www.Persnickety-Press.com

SUMMER ON EARTH

Peter Thompson

Acknowledgements

I would like to thank the many people who made this book possible. First, to Naomi Peralta, who added so much and helped make this story possible, thank you. To my early readers including Ron Edison and Brian Moore, two great readers and writers. A big thank you to my amazing agent Anna Olswanger, who saw how to make the story deeper and better, and always had faith. Thank you also to Susan Pearson for the excellent editing and Brian Sockin for making this book a reality. -- P.T.

Before

It was hotter than usual that night, and Grady couldn't get comfortable, even with the fan on high. The June bugs thumped against the window screen, and the crickets chirped so loudly it sounded like they were right there in the room. He could hear the TV on downstairs, so he knew Ma was still awake. Ever since Dad died she'd stayed up late most every night.

Grady just stared out the window and looked at the night sky. Where they lived, out in the country, there wasn't much light at night and the stars stood out more than they did in the city. Grady tried to find the constellations his Dad had taught him, just letting his mind wander. At some point he started to get sleepy. But before he fell asleep, he saw a shooting star. And when he saw it, he made a wish.

This is the story of how that wish came true.

.1.

Ralwil Turth

Intergalactic Year 465009.2053

To anyone watching the Midwestern night sky, it looked like a meteor that arced across the sky in a flash of bright light, then disappeared as it fell to earth. But inside the pod, Ralwil Turth was gripped with fear as he tried to control the path of his ship. He had been on his way home from a routine mining expedition on the outskirts of the Andromeda system, when the lights on his control board flashed in the urgent warning pattern. This signaled a breakdown of his primary power plant. His major energy source was draining fast. Without hesitation he switched to the spare power source.

The spare would not take him far. He had to find a place to bring his craft down to make the repair, and he didn't have any time to waste. Ralwil's body shook as he brought his universal map up on the view-screen. He was on the far side of the charted universe, light-years away from any known civilization. The information about this sector was old, but it showed that the third planet out in the nearest solar system was water-based and had an atmosphere rich in oxygen. It was the kind of place capable of *supporting* life, though according to the maps, there was no record of intelligent life in this quadrant. With no time to spare, he made the decision and aimed for the planet.

He cut the engine back and slowed down as he approached. His pod shuddered when he hit the atmosphere. The friction was intense, and the heat sensors flashed a warning. His styrpump beat madly against his chest and his brain felt as if it was going to explode. The pod's shields were designed to withstand tremendous heat, so if the systems worked properly he would be protected. But he had never had to test the systems. He hoped they worked better than the power source. The pod shook and screeched as if the ship was about to rip apart.

Ralwil tried to ignore his fear as he went through the emergency procedures. The vibrations increased and his whole body trembled. It felt as if his skelfones were going to shake right out of his body. He had never been this frightened before. It was hard to think, but he had to maintain control. He flipped on his personal force field. A cushion of cool air surrounded him and suddenly he was still again. He held his breath as he checked his view screen and searched for a safe place to land.

The image of the planet came up. He was above a large land mass. Scattered over the land were pockets of light, some small, others spread out in big clusters. Light meant energy, and concentrations like this didn't appear naturally. These lights were almost surely cities of some kind.

More bad luck! The planet had intelligent life forms after all!

This complicated his plan. Now he would have to work around the occupants without interfering with them in any way—if he survived.

Ralwil had to somehow coax his crippled machine down to a safe landing. He concentrated on the screen in front of him, steering toward the center of the land mass. It would not do to come down in the middle of one of their cities. The smart thing would be to land on the outskirts, somewhere where he could get his bearings and find the materials he needed without causing any alarm. He steered away from the main concentration of lights to a dark area between two small clusters. Moving fast, he dropped closer to the ground.

As he neared land, he shifted the image on the view screen to show the area in heat-sensitive infrared. At night, the heat map picked up surface features and life forms better than a visual map. The area was flat and appeared to be covered with plant life. A narrow strip cut through, winding around in a series of smooth curves. The temperature there was much cooler than in the surrounding area. It had to be water. Suddenly a new alarm went off and the screen flashed a warning. The power was almost drained. He cursed the makers of spare power supplies as he dipped his pod down closer to the ground. He set the controls for an automatic landing near the water, held his breath, and prepared to touch down.

He expected to glide in for a soft landing, but without warning his power supply gave way completely. The pod dropped like a stone and bounced once before stopping.

He felt a big bump, and then a shudder as his ship came to a rest.

His styrpump pounding, he took in a deep breath and tried to focus. He had survived! Ralwil slowly let his breath out and silently gave thanks.

The pod lights were dim and the only sound was the hum of the ventilation system. The power plant was out so he couldn't take off in his pod. His systems still worked off the reserve battery, but this would not last long. He would need to conserve his supply.

From now on, the ship's power could only be used for emergencies.

Ralwil picked up his onmibelt and made sure it was fully operational. His life depended on this thin belt. It held an assortment of tools and instruments. With this belt, and a little luck, he had a chance to survive on this alien planet. No, he thought, make that a lot of luck.

Before opening the pod's hatch, he took a reading of the outside air. It was a mixture of oxygen, nitrogen and more than a touch of methane. Not exactly what he was used to at home, but still breathable without additional gear. He pushed a button and the pod doors slid open.

Stepping out, he heard a sharp metallic chirping sound, mixed with a deeper bass. His first thought was that he was near some kind of strange machine. He touched a button on his and a holographic image appeared in front of him, showing the source of the noise.

The chirping came from thousands of little six-legged, winged creatures spread across the field, all rubbing their legs together. The deeper sounds were from two small cold-blooded creatures on opposite sides of the water's edge. He doubted that either of these species had the brain capacity to be intelligent, but their exotic nature was a marvel.

He touched another button as he shut the pod doors, and the pod disappeared from view. The invisi-shield would drain the batteries more than he would like, but it was a valuable protection from nosy natives. If a creature happened by and saw the ship, it would lead to problems. It was better not to be seen.

Ralwil sniffed the air around him. Its chemical makeup was safe to breathe, but the smell was atrocious. He wondered how these creatures could tolerate this noxious air, but he had no choice. If he didn't get out and explore, he would never be able to fix his power source and go home.

He walked up a small incline and was immediately in a field of tall leafy vegetation. Each plant was spaced evenly apart. On his native planet, Ralwil was considered unnaturally tall. At nearly three fornos, he towered over all the brothers in his swarm. But these plants were taller. He tried to look through them, but all he saw were more plants. Even the stars above were hidden by the leaves.

The chirping sound of the tiny winged creatures was so loud here it was hard to think. He kept on walking. The vegetation was everywhere. The leaves above him formed a canopy, cutting off the moonlight. He could hardly see in front of him. The leaves scraped against his outer membrane and gave him a creepy ticklish sensation. His styrpump beat faster. He was afraid he would panic if he did not get out in the open soon. *No—he had a mission to accomplish. He must not panic.* He fumbled at his belt, found his sensomap and took a reading. From its holographic sensor, he saw that there was an opening to the field off to the right. With relief, he turned and headed toward it.

As he got closer, his sensomap showed a hot spot—something large and slow moving, just past the edge of the field. It was obviously a life form, and it was clearly large enough to be intelligent. He could not show himself in his present form without causing all sorts of problems. He switched the setting on his belt to rough duplication mode. The instrument could send a wave of energy over the being, then re-form the wearer's molecular structure into a rough copy. Back home the tool was good for nothing much except practical jokes, but on expeditions it often came in handy. If he transformed himself into something like this native creature, it might be possible to get in close enough to do a synch-link.

He turned the duplicator on as he stepped out of the field. He felt a ticklish sensation as his molecules rearranged in the pattern of the being before him. It was a large quadrapodal creature with a long face and a huge swollen stomach. Its skin was thick, and, though light colored, there were big splotches of dark pigment throughout. It stood behind a barrier of some kind and stared at him with dull brown eyes.

Ralwil attempted a synch-link, but as he synched in with the creature's brain, all he could think about was how hungry he was, and how tasty the ground-covering vegetation looked. He swatted at a small flying creature with his tail and stepped back before the synch could progress any farther. He shivered. This creature was surely not intelligent. In fact, it appeared to be as dumb as wyr-tack. He reversed the duplicator and returned to his normal appearance. The creature vocalized with a loud mooing sound, then bent down to eat the vegetation on the ground.

Ralwil walked away from the creature and continued his exploration. His fear began to fade. He felt calmer now, almost excited about the adventure. The temperature was comfortable, the heat and humidity ratio nearly perfect. This was very pleasant. In a way, it reminded him of the equatorial regions on his home planet. The quality of light from the moon above was pleasing, and the stars shone brightly with a set of constellations he had never seen before. Even the noxious smell he had noticed before didn't seem so bad now. He couldn't believe he had adjusted to it so quickly. The life forms were exotic here too. Under different circumstances he would consider it interesting to spend some time here.

He came to a large structure made of organic material connected together in overlapping strips. The structure was easily twelve times as wide as his space pod, and twice as tall as it was wide. The two sides of its roof came together in a sharp peak. Ralwil recognized this as a primitive way of dealing with rain water.

With more efficient materials such architecture was not necessary, but it looked functional. Two large openings on the front came together to form an entrance. He walked over and looked up at the lock. It was a finely tooled metallic latch. The design was simple, but the detail required fine motor movement, or at least some kind of digital manipulation. This meant the creatures who built this must have hands. Based on the height of the lock, they walked upright, so most likely they were bipodal life forms, not so different from him, though obviously much larger.

He continued exploring and soon found more evidence of the native creatures. This was another structure, slightly smaller than the first but more ornate, with finer detail in the organic material, and openings covered with a transparent substance where the creatures could look out. This might be their living quarters, Ralwil thought. If so, he must be very careful that no one saw him. He skirted around the edge of the structure and checked his heat sensor.

It picked up four heat sources that appeared to be living creatures. Two of them were on higher levels of the structure, one near its peak, another near its midpoint. The last two were down at the structure's base, around the corner from where he stood. Of the two on the bottom, one was the largest, the other the smallest of the four.

Being so close was dangerous. The smart thing to do would be to back off and find a way to observe these creatures from a distance. Before approaching any unknown creatures, it was important to learn their habits and social functions, find out how they lived so he could determine if they were dangerous or not. Still, he had an overwhelming desire to get in close and see what these creatures looked like. What was the harm in that?

All he had to do was move in for a quick peek.

Ralwil kept close to the side of the structure and moved slowly around the corner, wondering what he would find next.

.2.

Grady
1978

That night, Grady dreamed he was lost in a deep forest. His family went to Wisconsin for vacation, and the dream reminded him of the forest there, only deeper and darker. He wandered around among the trees, but as much as he walked, the forest never ended. The trees were close together and all he could see in any direction were more trees. He could hardly see the sky above because of the thick leaves. Grady wasn't really scared, but he felt lonely. He wished someone was with him, someone who knew what to do and would help him get out of this forest.

And then he heard a voice. At first it was so soft that he couldn't even tell what it was saying. But as he walked toward it, it got louder and easier to understand. He still couldn't tell exactly what it was saying, but he thought he could make out some of the words, and somehow he knew that if he followed, the voice would lead him out into the clear.

He kept walking and as he listened, he realized it was Dad's voice. He started to run, wanting to catch up with his Dad. But as he ran, the voice started to fade. And then it stopped. He stood still and listened, straining to hear, but the voice was gone. He ran as fast as he could in the direction it had come from, but the only sounds he heard were of his own breathing and his own footsteps. He stopped again. Now he felt even more alone.

He knew he would never hear Dad's voice again.

Grady woke with a start, sweaty and breathing heavily. His heart raced. He felt like he really had been running in that forest. He took a big drink of water from the cup on his nightstand and tried to relax. It was still dark outside and the air was calm. The bugs thumped against the window screen just like before, and he could hear the TV downstairs. He wasn't a little kid anymore, so he knew it had just been a bad dream, but his room was so dark, and he knew Ma was still up. He got out of bed and headed down.

The lights were off in the living room and the only light was from the TV. The volume was turned up loud. He was surprised because whenever he and Luanne turned the volume up, Ma would come in and turn it way down. She told them they would ruin their hearing like that.

Ma was sitting on the big sofa with her back to Grady, and he didn't think she'd heard him come down. The TV was tuned to some old movie, but her head was down. It didn't look like she was even watching. He was about to speak, but something happened on the TV and he stood still for a minute and watched.

Ma jerked her head up and made a sound, a sob. She was crying. Ma hardly ever cried. She did when Dad died, of course. But when Grady and Luanne got sad, she was the one who helped them see that life was going to get better and that Dad would always be with them, in their hearts at least.

"Ma?" Grady said. "Are you all right?"

She didn't look back. With the TV so loud she didn't even hear him. He thought about going around the sofa and giving her a big hug and telling her that he loved her.

But he couldn't. He didn't want to see his Ma cry, and he didn't think she wanted him to see her like that. He turned around and headed back upstairs.

Back in his bed he stared out the window at the night sky. Grady wondered if their lives would ever get back to the way they were before.

.3.

Ralwil Turth

Ralwil walked around to the front of the structure. He had to climb up three raised levels to get to the entranceway platform. This too was made of organic material, with a stiff coating that was starting to peel off. The entranceway door was more than twice as tall as he was—more proof that giant creatures lived here. Next to the entranceway was another large opening covered with the transparent material. The structure had seemed dark, but as he got closer, he saw a soft glow coming from inside. He cautiously moved in closer.

Ralwil positioned himself at the edge of the transparent barrier and observed the interior. Lying on the floor, curled up in a semicircle, was a creature not much larger than himself. It was covered with fuzz, and its body moved up and down in a regular pattern. This had to be the small life form he had seen on the infra-red screen, but it was too small to be responsible for the buildings. Besides, it appeared to be a quadruped, and he doubted if it walked upright. Still, it was possible this creature was intelligent. Next to the creature stood a large straight-backed fixture covered in what looked like a soft material, patterned with a design that looked like a form of plant life. Beyond that stood a small box-shaped object, the source of the glow.

He pressed up close to the transparent barrier and stared at the box. Pictures moved across its screen in disjointed motion. The display was small and two dimensional, but the colors were bright and the image sharp. The technology seemed primitive compared to what he was used to, but it was fascinating nevertheless. The machine was evidently some sort of communicator, or maybe an instructional device.

Everything appeared tiny on the small box, but based on the size of the doorway and the layout of the structure, he was able to estimate the true scale. The box showed an image of a city with buildings of gleaming metal and more of the transparent substance, tall enough to reach the clouds. There were strange vehicles in a variety of shiny colors, one following another, stretched out to the horizon.

Watching the images flow across the box, Ralwil felt nostalgic for the cities on his home planet. He remembered the frenzies at the equinox, when the swarms came together to celebrate, and how hard it was to move without crawling all over one another. He missed the crowds, but he had jumped at the chance to travel the galaxies. He enjoyed the solitude of space, and the chance to experience other civilizations, however strange, bizarre, and exotic they might be.

The image on the screen changed. Now it showed a wide-open expanse with fields of vegetation rolling uninterrupted over great distance. This seemed like the area he was in now. He shifted anxiously as the image on the box focused on what had to be one of the native creatures. This creature was similar to, yet grotesquely different from, his species. Like him, it walked upright on two limbs, and one side of its body was a mirror image of the other.

There were similarities, but the differences were astounding. This creature was tall, with a big helmet of fuzz growing out of its head, and a complete absence of pigment in its skin. Its facial features jutted out in sharp angles, and its teeth were a gruesome white, like Wonk bones bleached in the sun. The creature was big, and one of the ugliest he had ever seen. But he could not look away from it. The creature looked revolting, but among its own kind, this specimen might be considered attractive.

He adjusted the duplicator settings on his omnibelt. The duplicator was designed to deal with fully dimensional, living creatures, and he had never tried it on a flat image. But in theory, it could work. The duplicator would take the data points it already had, along with the information about scale that Ralwil had learned from observation, make allowances for the rest, and the result would be a good, if not perfect, copy of the real creature. He locked in on the image and activated the duplicator. He felt a ticklish sensation as his atoms were rearranged in a pattern roughly equal in outward appearance to the creature in the box. He was much taller now, and the new fuzz on his head felt hot and itchy.

Being taller he could see the box better now. He noticed that the image had changed again. Now there was a different creature on the screen, even taller and wider than the other. This creature had no fuzz on its head, just a smooth skull that reflected light back in a soft shine. The look appealed to Ralwil.

He aimed the duplicator and activated it again. The ticklish sensation passed through his body and he fought the urge to giggle. Then he felt his form take its new shape, and he realized how big he was. He felt like a giant, clumsy and cumbersome. With a body this large, he wondered how he could control its movement. He took a step away from the window and a piece of the organic material under his feet made a creaking sound.

Maybe this was not such a good idea after all. The glowing box was fascinating, and he wanted to learn more about these creatures, but getting in so close was risky. It could be dangerous to assume their shapes when he really knew nothing about these creatures or how they lived. Besides, the interplanetary rules of alien contact were strict. If they found out at headquarters that he had made contact with an unauthorized species, his career would surely be finished. He would be disgraced. He had come to this planet for one reason: to fix the power source on his pod. He had no time to waste on risky games. He took another step backward.

He was about to exit the platform when he heard a fearsome snarling sound. It sounded like the noise the Gortuntugan engineer had made when he got his hand stuck in the static gears back on the Bornoxian expedition. Ralwil took another step back. He had been so caught up in watching the images on the box that he hadn't paid attention to the creature lying on the floor inside. Now it had put its head up against the transparent barrier and was staring straight at him and making that awful sound.

Ralwil felt his air passageway restrict with fear. He took another step backward, but in his new larger shape he was clumsy and awkward. He was afraid that he would trip and fall. Maybe if he were back in his real form, he could deal with this. He fiddled with the omnibelt, but his hands shook so much that he fumbled on the clasp and it came undone.

The belt clattered to the floor. It was small and compact, its width little more than a thin chain. But his best tools and instruments were on the belt, a technology light-years ahead of what these creatures were capable of. He reached down to pick it up, but he saw another flash of movement from behind the transparent barrier. Something was rising up, out of the straight backed fixture. It had to be one of the native creatures. If this creature saw him, then he would be in real trouble. Without pausing to think, he launched himself off the platform and landed in some scrunchy, scratchy vegetation.

The barking was more insistent now. Then he heard another sound, the sound of the door being unlocked. He willed himself to be still, and held his breath as he waited.

"What's a matter, girl? Something out there?"

Ralwil listened to the voice, but it was in a language he had never heard before.

The voice was soft and in a higher frequency than the barking. It almost felt soothing.

"Probably some old raccoon. You wouldn't know what to do with it if you caught it. Would you, Ruthie?"

The smaller creature kept up its noise, but now it seemed more like whining. Nearly shaking with fear, Ralwil wanted to raise his head up to get a good look at the new creature, but he didn't dare. He stayed still and tried not to move even though the vegetation poked at his outer membrane in a most irritating way. The smaller creature continued to whine urgently.

"Fine. You want out? Go on."

Ralwil heard a clicking sound, then a scurrying as the creature ran loose on the platform. Ralwil curled into a ball and waited for the attack. The scurrying came fast, then suddenly stopped at the edge of the platform, not far from where Ralwil lay. He heard a sniffing sound, close to him. Then, just as he was sure the creature would pounce, it let out a yelp and scurried backwards.

"See? It's nothing. You want back in?"

Ralwil pulled together all his courage and raised his head just enough to see over the platform. The small creature scooped up his omnibelt in its mouth just before it hurried inside the opened door. Ralwil caught a flash of a bare, unpigmented arm. Then the door closed, followed by another heavier door. Then he was all alone again, outside on this new planet. And all the tools he needed to survive were inside with these strange creatures.

.4.

Grady

At breakfast the next morning, Luanne wouldn't stop talking. She went on and on about some doll she'd seen on TV, and how she was going to die if Ma didn't buy it for her. Grady tried to ignore her while he reread an old comic book and ate his pancakes. Pancakes used to be a treat. But after Dad died, they'd stopped buying breakfast cereal from the store because it was too expensive. Now every morning it was either oatmeal or pancakes with thin syrup. After a while he started to hate pancakes.

Luanne kept on with her whining. It made it real hard to read, and Grady was already in a bad mood from the night before. Ma wasn't saying much, probably because she felt bad about not being able to buy the doll. It bothered him that Luanne was making Ma feel bad. Finally he'd had about all he could take.

"Shut up!" Grady yelled. "Shut up about the stupid doll!"

Luanne stopped in mid-sentence. In fact, it seemed like all the noise in the kitchen stopped. Ma had been rinsing the dirty dishes. Maybe she'd turned off the water, or maybe not, but all of a sudden the only thing Grady could hear was his own breathing.

Then Luanne started to cry, just like he knew she would.

"Mommm! Grady's yelling at me!" She shoved her plate away, knocking over the jar of syrup. He watched as the syrup spilled across the table, running over the wood like a sticky river. He didn't even think to pick up the jar.

Ma brushed a strand of her long blond hair out of her eyes and took a deep breath. She was thin and pale, and she didn't look strong enough to do much of anything. But looks were deceiving. In her own way she was strong, and Grady could never get anything past her. She didn't yell. She never yelled. But he could tell she was upset. She grabbed a rag from the sink and started wiping up the syrup. Luanne was now crying loud enough to wake the dead. Ma picked up the syrup jar and turned toward Grady, her eyes set hard. He knew the look. She was ready to give it to him. She hardly ever raised her voice, but she always made her position clear. He didn't wait for her to start, though. He was still wound up, and he let loose again at Luanne.

"She's not going to buy you the stupid doll," he yelled. "She's not going to buy it because we don't have any money. Don't you know anything?"

"Grady!" Ma's voice was sharp. "Stop it right now."

Grady looked away. He knew as soon as he'd said it, that it was the wrong thing to say. But he was still glad he'd said it.

Luanne screamed louder.

"And you stop it too, Luanne, or you'll be inside scrubbing floors for the rest of the morning."

Luanne whimpered, but she stopped crying. Ma didn't make empty threats. When she said something, she meant it, and it was too nice a day to stay inside. Grady took a deep breath and waited for his turn. But Ma didn't even look at him. She wiped up all the syrup and went back to the sink, where she ran the water and squeezed out the rag.

Grady knew that what he'd said was true, but it was over the line. His stomach tightened as he waited for Ma to say something. But she didn't say a word. She came back and wiped the table again with the clean rag. He thought that maybe he should apologize, but he didn't want to say the words.

Then Ma spoke, quietly but firmly, an edge of disappointment in her voice. "It's getting late, Grady. You better go on out and do your chores."

"Yes, ma'am." He bounded up from the chair, put his dirty dishes in the sink, and headed outside as quickly as he could. The sun was already moving up in the sky, and it felt like it was going to be another hot day. He kicked up dust as he walked and shooed away a couple of big flies. It felt good being outside, away from Luanne's whining and Ma's disappointment. He probably shouldn't have said anything, he thought, but he was mad. And besides, it was the truth. They didn't talk about money much in their family. Ma always kept her problems to herself. But it didn't take a genius to know they were in trouble. Everybody knew they were.

It had been about a week or so after Dad died, while the church ladies were still bringing over casseroles every night, that Mr. McAfferty had come by to visit. Mr. McAfferty worked at the bank, but he'd gone to school with Dad, and they'd known each other for years. They used to stop in his office whenever they went into town, and Mr. McAfferty always gave Grady and Luanne candy to eat while he and Dad went over business.

That night, Mr. McAfferty came by wearing a fancy three-piece suit. It had been raining all week, and he had mud splatters all over his shiny black shoes. Ma invited him in, and they spent a long time in the living room, talking real low. Grady stayed with Luanne in the kitchen, helping her with her homework, while they talked.

Grady could see the banker from the kitchen as he got ready to go. He seemed upset as he put on his overcoat. Just before leaving, he shook his index finger at Ma and scolded her. "You're a proud woman, Helen, but this pride is going to bring you down. If you don't listen to reason, don't blame me for what I've got to do."

After he left, Ma got down on her hands and knees and wiped up all the mud he'd tracked in.

After that, Grady heard some comments at school. Joey Thorsen asked him where they were going to go after they lost the farm. He told him they weren't going to lose it, but Joey said his parents had talked about it over dinner, and they said they were. Grady called him a liar, but even though he said it, he knew Joey was right, and he was worried about what was going to happen to their family. They were just about ready to fight about it when the teacher broke them up.

Grady took his time walking out to the barn. He had a lot more chores to do since Dad died, but it was summer and he had all day to get them done. Some of the things, like milking Dora, had to be done right away. Other things he could put off longer. He stopped by the back of the house where a big anthill had formed near the foundation. He poked at the hill with a stick for a while and watched all the ants scurrying out as they tried to figure out what was going on. That's how he felt sometimes, since Dad died. Like he was one of those ants, and he didn't know what to do, but he had to do something quick or the whole world was going to fall down on him. After a few minutes, he stopped poking and headed back to the barn to do his chores.

He was still thinking about what had happened at breakfast and not paying attention when he came to the barn. He'd already started to pull the big door open before he noticed that the lock was undone. That seemed strange. He'd locked it up the night before, and no one had been out yet that morning. Maybe he didn't lock it up after all, he thought, but that didn't seem likely. Once, a long time back, he'd forgotten. Dad had given him a real tongue lashing, and after that, he always double checked before he went in for the night.

He pulled the door all the way open now and cautiously looked inside. The barn was dark and smelled like hay and diesel fuel. Their big old tractor was up front, right where it was supposed to be. Off to the side was a wooden work bench loaded with tools. Next to it was a tall shelving unit jammed full of cans of oil and transmission fluid, and jars of strangely colored mixtures, each labeled with a piece of masking tape. As far as he could tell, nothing looked out of place. It felt real creepy, though, thinking that some-one had been here. Maybe they were here now, maybe even hiding and watching him. Their farm was out far enough that they didn't see other people very often. They were miles from town, and bordered on each side by the fields of other farmers. The mailman came by every day, and Mr. or Mrs. Pratchet from down the road stopped by a few times a week to see if there was anything they could do to help Ma. But most of the time it was just the family.

He slowly walked around the tractor and looked toward the other side of the barn. Several big drums of fertilizer and herbicide stood in a row. Beyond them was a pyramid formed with bales of hay. Nothing was out of place. He had almost convinced himself that nothing was wrong. Then he looked at the back door. On the side wall, right next to the door, Dad had hung a pair of big overalls that he'd worn when he worked on the tractor. The overalls were gone.

Now he felt kind of creeped out, but at the same time excited. He knew he should go tell Ma, but he didn't want to just yet. This was a mystery, like the in the old Hardy Boys books he'd found in the attic. Something was going on, and he wanted to be the one to find out what it was.

He went out the back door and into the pen where they kept Dora at night. She was standing off in the corner with her head to the ground, munching away. She barely glanced at him as he walked through. Grady looked at the ground, searching for clues, and he found one right away. As Dora walked around eating, she did her business right on the ground. The pen had a fresh pile of poop close by the doorway. But the pile was flattened in a way that looked like it had been stepped in. Grady looked closer, and he was sure of it. A little bit farther on, the grass was dirty from where someone had scraped the stuff off his foot. That was at the edge of the pen, the side leading down toward the creek. Grady ducked under the fence and headed down toward it.

He walked along the edge of the cornfield, bent over like he'd seen them do in the movies when they were sneaking up on someone. The corn was up just past waist level now and if someone was watching, Grady was clearly visible. Grady walked all the way to the edge of the field where it ended at the creek near the back end of their property.

The land beyond was several acres of wild brush: a mix of tall grasses, bramble bushes and willow trees. Grady knew where all the blackberry bushes were, and he'd spent a lot of afternoons exploring the area. He'd never find anyone hiding there. So he stayed on this side of the creek.

Grady kept to the edge of the field, moving slowly along the creek. He was pretty excited by now, wondering who it was who'd broken into their barn. Maybe it was a hobo, maybe even an escaped convict. The more he thought about it, the surer he was that it was some criminal he was tracking down. There was probably a reward on his head. If he captured him, he'd give the reward money to Ma. He would save the farm, and he'd get his picture in the paper and everyone would know he was a hero.

He pushed some weeds out of the way and stepped around the corner of the cornfield. The man was sitting right there, wearing Dad's overalls, holding something in his hands. Grady froze. The man was big, and bald-headed, and looked different from anyone that Grady knew. This man wasn't from anywhere around here. Grady looked into his eyes, and he wasn't sure who was more scared, him or the man he'd just found.

.5.

Ralwil Turth

Ralwil was sitting by the water, close to where he had hidden his pod, when a new creature snuck up and surprised him. His mouth dropped open in shock as he stared up at the intruder. This was not the one he had seen last night. This one seemed smaller, and there wasn't nearly as much fuzz on its head. But it was surely of the same family grouping. Ralwil's body throbbed, and he found it hard to breathe. The creature stared at him with its eyes wide open. Ralwil had the urge to get up and run, but in this big, clumsy body, he didn't know how far he could get before falling. This creature would surely capture him. Then it would find the pod and all would be lost. How had he gotten himself into such a mess?

The creature stood still, its eyes and mouth wide open in what looked to him like a fierce display of aggression. Ralwil braced himself and waited for it to attack, but the creature did not move. They both stayed still for a long moment. Had he misinterpreted its intentions? Now that he looked enough like them, he could think of no reason for this creature to be aggressive toward him. As far as the creature knew, he was one of them.

What did these creatures do when they met one another? He had no idea of how to act. His only hope was to get close enough to this creature to do the synch-link.

He started to push himself up. The creature moved back a step.

The creature was afraid of him too!

Ralwil slowly slid in the opposite direction. The creature cautiously moved a step forward. He did it again, and the creature moved another step closer. It raised its hands and made some kind of strange vocal sound. The words made no sense, but the voice sounded low and soothing. Ralwil stayed still and the creature moved another small step closer. Ralwil's styrpump beat fast against his chest like the timing mechanism on an old qkartagraph. He was afraid, but this creature was so exotic and interesting. He wanted to find out more about it.

The creature took another step forward, then stopped. It was still a couple of body lengths away, just out of reach. Ralwil relaxed his mind and sent out a comfortable welcome vibration. The expression on the creature's face changed. He took another step forward. Now the creature was within reach.

Before the thing was able to try anything aggressive, Ralwil changed his own brainwave configuration and started the synch with the creature's brain waves.

Ralwil let the feelings flow. Images flashed across his mind. As if looking from above, he saw wide fields of open vegetation, all growing a type of food crop, and the name of the crop came into his mind. They called it *corn*. Now he was viewing things from the creature's living area. He lived high up in the structure Ralwil had seen the night before, and the area he looked over was called a *farm*. This farm belonged to the creature's family grouping, and he had lived there all his life. Images of flames, eleven of them, came into his mind, burning brightly on top of a white platform.

Then, looking through the creatures eyes, he blew the flames out and felt a rush of joy. This had a name too. This was a *birthday*, a celebration of the anniversary of his birth, and the flames he blew out were called *candles*. People around him raised their voices in a melodic song, and Ralwil flushed with pride as they sang to honor him. This creature was young, he realized. He was just a pup. And the creature he had seen before, the tall one with the fuzzy head— no, not fuzz, it was called *hair*—hugged him, and he felt a strong emotion, stronger than any he ever felt before, and it was called *love*.

Next he was outside, lying in the sun, watching the clouds above him drift across the sky. A contented, lazy feeling washed over him, and he felt himself curl his lips upward in what he knew to be a *smile*. Other images, sounds, and smells rolled over him. He tasted something bitingly cold, but sweet and flavorful, a small taste of paradise, and the name came to him. They called it *ice cream*. He saw people's faces and the names attached to them, and found that, although they all looked similar, he could distinguish among them. He saw other creatures they called *animals*: *cows, horses, ducks*, and the creature that had chased him the night before, a *dog*. His mind marveled at the fullness of this life.

The picture changed again. He was in a large, dimly lit room filled with people. He knew most of them in one way or another. They were all watching him as he walked up to the front of the room. He stopped by a long box made out of shiny organic material he now knew was called *wood*. Inside the box, a man lay with his arms crossed over his chest and his eyes closed. The love emotion welled up again, and he knew that this was the young creature's father.

Then a new emotion flowed through him, just as strong as the one called love, only this one shook his whole body and brought water to his eyes. This one was labeled sadness, or *grief,* and he knew that the father had died. Ralwil knew of death, of course, but in his culture it was something to be celebrated. Death was just the end of one phase of life and the beginning of another. But this feeling was too strong, too raw. He felt a wrenching in his gut, and he pulled away.

Ralwil gasped for breath. The creature—no, the *boy,* he was a boy human—stood in front of him and blinked his eyes dazedly. This was a natural reaction after a first synch-link. The boy would not remember any of it later. It would seem like a dream. Now Ralwil understood him, and much, much more about how these creatures thought and lived. He felt a connection with the boy like he had not felt since leaving his home planet.

Ralwil's body surged with the emotion. All he could think

about was the incredible sadness, and how he wished he could do something to help this boy.

.6.

Grady

Ma was naturally suspicious of strangers, and out in the country as far as they were, not many came around. So that day, when Grady found Will down by the creek, he knew he wasn't supposed to talk to him. But he did, and somehow he got a real good feeling about him. So he took him up to see Ma. She was out back by the barn, trying to get the tractor started, but all it did was turn over and belch out this thick black smoke. Ever since Dad died, she'd been taking on most of the farm duties by herself, and Grady knew she was having a hard time keeping up. She was sitting up in the cab, but she had the top up, so the engine was showing. The tool box was out. It looked like she'd been playing around with the engine before they got there. Grady tried to get her attention, but she was concentrating on what she was doing and didn't notice as they came up.

Grady glanced over at Will. He had this intense look on his face as he stared at the engine. It was funny. Even though Grady had just met him, he already felt comfortable with him, as if he'd known him all his life. Down by the creek, he'd been stalking him, thinking he was a robber, trying to capture him. Then, he wasn't sure how, they'd just started talking and he knew he was okay. He was different from all the other people he knew. It wasn't just the way he looked, though that was part of it. He couldn't explain it, but Will seemed almost like a kid in that big old body. Right away Grady knew they were going to be friends. Will didn't talk much, and when he did, he spoke in a deep voice, but real slowly, like he wasn't sure he was using the right words. Now he was staring at the engine as it turned over again, his forehead scrunched up like he was thinking.

"Gosh darn it!" Ma yelled from up in the cab. Now Grady knew she hadn't seen him. She never cursed in front of the kids, and this was pretty close to a curse for her.

Will stared at the engine for another second, then reached

into the toolbox and grabbed a vice grip and a long screwdriver. Ma turned over the engine again as he reached in, and Grady thought it was going to start up and catch Will's arm. "Stop!" he yelled as loud as he could.

Ma must have heard him, because she stopped right away. She leaned out of the cab. "Grady? What's going on? What are you doing here?"

He was about to answer, but Will was bent over the engine compartment, twisting something with the vice grip. Grady didn't know what he was doing, and he was afraid Will was going to break something.

Ma yelled down again. "Grady? What's going on down there?"

Will looked up at him with this real sincere look on his face. "Now."

"What?"

Will's face screwed up again as he tried to make himself clear. He pointed down at the engine. "Again. Now."

Grady finally got it. He hollered up at Ma again. "Try it again."

Ma leaned down over the side. She could see Grady, but Will

was under the engine hood and she couldn't see him. "What are you doing?" she asked.

"Come on, Ma. Just try it again." He didn't know why, but Grady felt sure that Will knew what he was doing.

Ma gave him a strange look, like she thought he was crazy, but she got back in the cab and turned the key again. This time it started right up. The engine caught on with a roar, then settled down to a smooth purr. It hadn't sounded as good as that since it was new. Ma revved the engine and it didn't sputter or cough. It sounded sweet and forceful. The smoke coming out the stack wasn't as thick either. Ma climbed down out of the cab.

"What did you do, Grady? I couldn't even get it to turn." Then she saw Will and stopped in mid sentence. Her whole body froze. Grady wished he'd warned her somehow. She recovered after a second.

"Hello," she said coolly. "I didn't realize we had company."

Grady cut in right away. "He fixed the engine, Ma. He's real good with fixing stuff."

He wasn't even sure why he'd said that, though he knew it was true.

Ma gave him a look. He knew she was upset, but she was too

polite to show it.

She turned to Will. "You fixed this?"

He didn't say anything, but he nodded his head.

She looked at the engine and listened to it for a moment as it purred away. "Well, thank you," she said. "That hasn't been running right for quite a while. I was afraid I was going to have to have someone come out and work on it. You're looking for work, I suppose?"

Will still didn't say anything, but he nodded his head again.

"I'm sorry, but I'm afraid I can't afford anyone now. I do wish you the best. The Johansen's, they live up the road on the way into town, they might need someone."

Will lowered his head. Grady cut in again. "We've got lots of things that need to be done, Ma. "

She shot him the look again. "I'm sorry. We just can't afford it now."

Will looked down at the ground for a moment. Then, in his deep slow voice he said, "Food?"

"You're hungry? Oh, well, of course we can feed you," she said. She looked uncertain, but then she looked him in the eyes and made a decision. "I guess there are a few things you can help with."

After that, Ma got Will a sandwich, then showed him how to do some work down in the south field. As the day went on, it began to heat up. By midmorning, Grady was hot and tired and just about finished with his chores, so he went into the house to get some water. When he came into the kitchen, Ma was on the phone. He listened to her talk as he got a glass out of the cupboard and ran the faucet to let the water get cold.

"No, sheriff, I don't think there's a problem." She was quiet as she listened. Grady filled up his glass and turned off the faucet. "Okay, if there's any trouble I'll give you a call. Thanks again. Goodbye." He took a long drink as she hung up the phone.

"That was Sheriff Reynolds," she said. "I called about this man you found, to see if he knew anything about who he was, or how he got here. He said that the canning plant down in Leland just closed down. There were some migrant workers who lost their jobs and have been drifting around the county. He thought Will might be one of them." She looked out the kitchen window to where Luann was playing in the dust, drawing pictures with a stick. "He seems okay to me, but after we feed him tonight, we're going to have to send him on his way."

"He seems real handy though, Ma. He could help out a lot."

"We don't even know who this man is, Grady. And besides, we can't afford to pay him. It's best to send him on his way." She was quiet for a bit before she spoke again. "It is sad to see a man hungry, though. He can stay, but just for dinner tonight."

.7.

Ralwil Turth

Being around the creatures, Ralwil quickly learned some of their habits and quirks. The one called Ma was clearly the head of their social structure. She was the one who provided the food and determined the work assignments. She was the one who held control of the family unit. He determined that she was a female of the species, and that this was most likely a female-dominated culture. He also realized that if he was going to be able to stay near his pod, and find the materials he needed to fix the power source, he would need to get her cooperation. He thought about doing a synch-link with her, but she was clearly a powerful being, and he did not want to risk her taking control of his mind and finding out who he really was. He had to be careful when he was around her.

Another thing he noticed as he got in close to these creatures, was the texture of their skin. They had small holes in their skin—very small holes, but visible enough—especially on their faces. When he had first used his omnibelt and duped into his current shape, he had done it based on the image in the glowing box. The automatic function had worked well, considering. But in this case, and maybe in others he had not figured out yet, it got the details wrong. It was mostly a matter of resolution. If he had gotten in closer, it might have worked better. If he had his omnibelt, he could easily fix it. But the belt was still inside their structure where the furry creature had taken it. He hoped they would not notice how different he looked before he could somehow manage to get into that structure—*house*, that was the word for it—and get his belt back.

Another thing he had not counted on was the amount of energy he expended inside this creature's form. With the larger body and increased musculature, he was burning energy at an astounding rate. The one called Ma had brought him some food made out of plant-based organic material. It tasted sweet and stopped the urgent growling in his stomach, but the texture was strange and sticky, and it stuck to the top of his mouth. It was truly exotic. He still was not sure if he liked it or not. At least it gave him enough energy to do the work the Ma assigned.

They were such simple tasks that once he was shown what he needed to accomplish, he quickly figured out more efficient ways to achieve the results. By the time he had finished the tasks, the sun had moved across the sky and he was in need of more energy again. So he felt a surge of joy when Grady came down to tell him that supper was ready and to come up to the house. This was a chance not only to get his energy replenished, but maybe find a way to get his belt back.

The inside of the house was different than he had expected. The floor was constructed of smooth slats of the organic material called wood, covered with soft fibrous coverings blended together in a colorful pattern. The ceiling was higher than his head, and there was room to spare, but somehow it still felt as comfortable and cozy as his pod. Grady led him into the kitchen, the room where the food was prepared. The Ma was standing in front of a large white object with her back toward him. His styrpump beat a little faster when he saw a blue flame come out of the object, but the Ma was standing close to it, and she did not seem concerned, so he thought it must be part of the food ritual. In the center of the room was a large circular wooden structure raised off the ground by four thin pedestals. He closed his eyes and the word came to him: *table.*

Containers of several different food items were scattered across it. There were four sitting stations—*chairs*—around the table, and one of them was occupied by a creature he hadn't seen before. This one was a small female, obviously just a pup. She stared at him with wide eyes.

"Supper's almost ready. You can wash up first," the Ma said, glancing back at him.

Ralwil stood still as he tried to understand the command. Then Grady came and pushed him forward toward a sunken area in the platform underneath the window.

"We can wash up in the sink," he said. He turned a knob and water came out of a long metallic tube. Grady reached his hands into the stream of water, then picked up a white object next to the sink and began rubbing it over his hands. Ralwil hesitated, waiting for him to finish, then he did the same. The water was cool and refreshing, and the white object felt slick in his hands. It bubbled up as he rubbed it over his skin. It was a delightful feeling, and he had the urge to laugh out loud.

"That's enough," Grady said. He handed him a strip of fabric.

Ralwil rubbed it over his hands like he had seen Grady do, and it dried his hands.

"Go ahead and sit down," the Ma said.

Grady sat down on the chair next to the smaller human and motioned Ralwil to sit next to him. Ralwil sat down. Steam drifted up from the containers on the table and he smelled a rush of different scents all at once. The smells were earthy and sweet, a dense perfume of unfamiliar aromas. He felt his stomach rumble with hunger.

The Ma sat down in the open chair. "Luanne, it's your turn to say grace."

The small human made a face, then lowered her head and put her hands together.

The others did the same, so Ralwil copied their motions.

"For food and drink and tender care we give thee thanks dear Lord and may Thou in our hearts and homes ever be adored Amen." She said it fast, with the words all rushed together, and Ralwil had no idea what she was saying.

"Grady, pass the potatoes, please," the Ma said.

Grady picked up a bowl filled with white fluffy stuff, scooped some of it onto his plate, then handed it to Ralwil. Ralwil held the bowl in his hand, not certain what to do with it. He watched as the Ma picked up another bowl, this one filled with long green things, put some on her plate, then passed it to the young creature. The young creature passed it on to Grady without taking any. She was still staring at him with her wide eyes. Ralwil passed the bowl on to the Ma without taking any. Other bowls were passed into his hands: the green things, a platter of brown stuff covered with a thick brown liquid, and another platter with thin slices of a white porous material with brown edges on the outside—it looked like the same stuff he'd eaten earlier. In each case, he passed the platters on without taking any. After everything had been passed around, the others all had their plates filled with food, though in the young creature's case there was hardly any. His plate was still empty.

Luanne, the young creature, looked at him and started laughing.

The Ma gave her a sharp look, and she stopped. Then the Ma turned toward Ralwil. "I'm sorry Mr. . . . Will. Aren't you hungry?"

Ralwil felt a panicky feeling in the pit of his stomach. Had he done something wrong with the eating ritual? Had he made an error? "Yes!" he said. "I am hungry." The Ma gave him a strange look, then nodded her head. "I'm sorry. Where are my manners?

Please help yourself to whatever you like. You do eat this kind of food, don't you?"

Ralwil froze. He had no idea if he ate this kind of food or not, but this was human food, so he had to eat it or they would know something was wrong. "Yes," he said.

"Don't be shy." The Ma scooped a heap of the white fluffy stuff onto his plate. "If you're hungry, just take what you need. This isn't fancy, but it's filling." She put some of the contents of each of the other bowls and platters onto his plate so that it nearly overflowed with the strange food. He looked over at Grady, who, without even looking up, was shoveling the food into his mouth with a metallic poker with four points at its end. The Ma turned away and carefully cut a piece of the brown stuff with the edge of her metallic poker. Luanne just moved the food around on her plate as she stared at him.

He picked up his poker and cautiously stuck it into the white mound. He scooped it up and slowly brought it up to his mouth. It felt strange sticking the poker in his mouth, and he tried to do it without injuring himself. The food was smooth and creamy with a mild starchy taste. He rolled it around in his mouth. It tasted strange, but not unpleasant.

He swallowed and scooped up another bite.

"I'm afraid I didn't get your full name before. Is Will your first name?" the Ma asked.

Ralwil's mouth was full of the white fluffy stuff. "Ralwil Turth," he answered, but with his mouth full, it didn't come out right.

The Ma looked confused, but she went right on. "Where are you from . . . Will? You're not from these parts, are you?"

Ralwil scooped up some more of the white substance. The more he tried it, the more he liked it. "No," he said.

The Ma hesitated a second, then asked another question. "I don't mean to pry, but we don't get many strangers coming by. I was just wondering how you came to be here. Are you from Iowa originally?"

Ralwil finished the last of the white stuff on his plate and took another big heap from the bowl. "No," he said. "Far away."

"I think he's a space alien!" Luanne, the small creature, cried out.

"Luanne!" The Ma's face turned red. "I'm sorry. She has quite an imagination. We don't see many . . . I mean, we don't get many strangers out here."

Ralwil took another bite of the white stuff—*potatoes*—he really liked these potatoes. He heard them talking around him, but he lost interest in listening. All he wanted to do was eat these fluffy, smooth potatoes. He sensed they were talking to him and he knew he had to say something, but he didn't know what he should say. Besides, his mouth was full so it was hard to talk.

"Hmmmph?" he said.

"I'm sorry?" The Ma was looking at him strangely again. Grady and Luanne were looking at him too. He felt his pulse quicken. Did he make a mistake with the food ritual again? This was all too complicated.

He was about to say something, he was not sure what, when he heard a growling noise behind him. It was the same sound he had heard the night before when he first came to examine the structure. The creature was at the edge of the room, right at the entranceway. It stood on its four legs, its fuzz up at the collar, and its teeth set in a fierce display.

"Ruthie! Stop it!" the Ma said in a commanding voice. But the creature did not stop. It took a step forward and barked, a loud aggressive sound.

Ralwil felt his styrpump race, but as he looked into the creature's eyes, he saw that it was old and scared. It did not seem so frightening.

"It's okay, Ruthie," Grady said in a soothing voice. "It's not you," he told Ralwil. "She doesn't like strangers and I think she just woke up."

Ralwil looked into the creature's eyes and sent out a calm wave of energy. The creature stopped barking, but it growled again. Ralwil began to worry. This creature had his omnibelt. If he had any hope of fixing the power source, he had to come to terms with it. It was at the edge of the room, but just within range to do a synch-link.

He locked in with the creature's brain waves and immediately felt the images flow. He was in a green field, running so fast that his heart felt like it would explode, but he felt a joy like he had never experienced before. He chased after fat-tailed gray creatures that scampered up the side of a tree just before he could catch them. He lived in a world of smells. Smells so dense and vibrant they were almost three dimensional. He felt his leg twitch as he sniffed around and learned how smells he had thought repulsive carried their own pleasure and knowledge. Then the love flowed again, though this was different from the love he had felt when he had synched with

Grady. This was a love for his keepers, a loyalty and trust that meant he would do anything to keep them safe. Then he felt the pain. He was old now, and his hip ached, and it hurt to run. Now he had no energy. All he wanted to do was sleep. Ralwil pulled back and disengaged his brain waves.

The creature stopped growling. Now it came forward, sniffing. Ralwil put his hand out and the creature, Ruthie, sniffed it. She made a soft whimpering sound and laid her head in his lap. Ralwil stroked her fur. It felt soft and smooth, a pleasant experience.

Luanne laughed. "Ruthie likes him."

"Why, I never . . . " the Ma said.

"She likes you," Grady said.

Then Ruthie raised her head, turned, and trotted from the room. Ralwil felt disappointed. He liked the warm sensation of her fur against his hand.

"Where's she going?" Grady asked.

Ralwil turned back to his supper. Then he heard the clackety-clack of Ruthie's nails against the wood floor. She ran right up to him and put her head in his lap again, but this time he felt her nudge something out of her mouth. He reached down under the table and felt the fine chain of his omnibelt. A wave of relief washed over him as his hand closed around it. He stroked Ruthie's head with his other hand, then looked back to see the Ma staring at him. Grady and Luanne were also looking at him.

Ralwil hesitated. He had already messed up once with the food ritual. Now it looked like he had made some other mistake, but he had no idea what it was. He patted Ruthie's head once more, then picked up his poker and scooped up another bunch of the white fluffy stuff. He swallowed it down before turning to the Ma.

"These are good . . . po-tat-oes," he said.

The Ma smiled. "Thank you," she said. "I'm so glad you like them."

.8.

Grady

The next morning started out hot. Ma cooked oatmeal for breakfast again. The air felt steamy before Grady even took a spoonful. They had fresh raspberries and cream with it so it tasted good, but for about the thousandth time he wished they had store-bought cereal again. He slumped over his bowl and ate without talking. Luanne was in a talkative mood though. He didn't know how she was able to eat oatmeal and talk at the same time, but she rambled on, hardly taking a breath.

"When I grow up I want to be a nurse, or maybe a doctor," she said. "It would be fun working in a hospital. Then I could wear white all the time."

"Uh-huh." Ma had only taken a few bites of her breakfast. She sat at the table working on some papers. Grady didn't think she was really listening.

"Maybe I'll live in a big city somewhere. I can come back home to the farm on weekends. And I'll be a pilot and get my own plane. That way I could go anywhere I want, anytime I wanted."

Grady ate his oatmeal and thought about what he would do today. He'd be done with his chores in a few hours. Then he'd have some free time. It was so hot, he thought he might go down to the creek. It was shady there, and he could fish or hunt crawdads. When it got too hot, he could just jump into the creek to cool down. Or maybe he'd head over to the swimming hole. He was paying no attention to Luanne, until she said, "Is Will going to stay with us, Ma?"

"Will?" Ma looked up from her papers. "No. He was just helping out yesterday, dear. I'm sure he has places to go. He probably has family somewhere."

"But what if he doesn't? Maybe he wants to stay here with us."

"Well, I don't think that's going to happen. He doesn't really fit in around here. It will be best for everyone if he just moves along."

Grady liked Will and hoped he would stay. But the way Ma spoke, he knew her mind was made up. Besides, what she said made sense. Will didn't really belong with them, and he had to have family or people who loved him somewhere.

"I like Will. I think he's nice." Luanne said as she twirled her spoon. "He talks funny though."

"Don't say that, Luanne. It's not polite," Ma put down her pen and paper and looked directly at Luanne. "He can't help the way he is."

"Why is he that way then?"

"Well, he's just a little bit slow. His brain works differently than yours."

Grady thought about that. He didn't think Ma had it right at all. Will was different. He could tell that right away by the way he walked and the way he talked. But he picked things up quickly and he seemed plenty smart to Grady. Will was just smart in a different way.

"I like him," Luanne said. She picked a raspberry out of her bowl and popped it into her mouth. "He makes me laugh."

They finished breakfast and cleaned everything up, then

headed out to do their chores. They found Will standing alongside the house, just staring up at the sky with a big smile on his face. Grady tipped his head up to see what he was looking at, but all he saw were a few puffy clouds in a clear blue sky. But the expression on Will's face was joyful, as if he was watching something really interesting, maybe even wonderful.

Luanne also looked up at the clouds. Then she started to giggle.

"What are you looking at, Will? Those are just some old clouds," said Grady.

"Clouds!" Will said. He kept staring up at the sky.

Luanne giggled again and looked back up at the sky.

Grady wondered what Will was seeing. The clouds didn't look like anything in particular, just cottony blobs. But the more he stared at them, the more beautiful they seemed. He'd seen clouds nearly every day of his life and never given them a second thought. Now he wondered how they were formed, and why these few were here in an otherwise open sky, and how wonderful it was to have clouds, and how empty the sky would be if they weren't there. It felt like he was looking at them for the first time.

"That one looks like a rabbit," Luanne said.

It did look kind of like a rabbit with part of one ear missing. Then the kitchen door opened and swung shut. Ma looked surprised that they were all looking up at the sky, but she didn't look up or say a word about it. She had a bag in her hand. She walked over and handed it to Will.

"Will, we really appreciate your help yesterday, but I'm afraid we can't afford to pay you. I've made some sandwiches for you. We wish you all the best."

Will looked in the bag. "Sand-wiches," he said.

"That's right," Ma said. "It's not much, but it will keep you from going hungry. Thank you again for helping yesterday."

Will smiled. But he stood rooted in his spot. It didn't look like he had any intention of going anywhere.

Ma stood waiting for a long moment. Then, with a puzzled look on her face, she headed off to the barn. "Grady, Luanne, let's go. We have chores to do."

Luanne skipped ahead and Grady followed. About halfway there, he looked back. Will was right behind him, heading to the barn with the rest of them. Ma looked back at the same time. She stopped, put her hands on her hips, and looked at Will.

"Will, I am sorry if I'm not making myself clear. I don't

have the money to pay you. You need to go somewhere else to find work."

"I find work here," Will said. He walked past her and headed into the barn.

Grady finished up his chores and spent most of the afternoon at the swimming hole over by the Clarkson's farm. On his way home he cut through the south field, where he found Will working on an irrigation pump. The south field was farthest away from the water tanks, and they needed pumps to get the water from the tanks to the field. It didn't rain much in the summer, so without the pumps working, the crops would dry out. The family always had problems with the pumps, and Dad had to replace a few every year.

Will sat on the ground surrounded by pieces of the pump he had taken apart. It looked like a jigsaw puzzle, only there were pieces of every shape and size. He held one up and turned it around, inspecting it from all sides. Then he picked up another piece and made the same close inspection.

Grady sat down on the ground next to him. He'd helped his Dad sometimes when he was working on things. He liked to see how things fit together, how all sorts of little parts could be assembled to make something that worked. He'd helped Dad rebuild a tractor engine once. It almost felt like magic when it all fit together and started up on the first try.

Will took one of the pieces and bent the narrow end of it a little. He looked at it closely, then used pliers to bend it even more. He picked up another piece and put it together with the first piece. They fit perfectly. He smiled and made a strange grunting sound. Grady watched Will work for a long time. Sometimes Will asked him to hand him a part or reach over for a tool he needed. It felt good to help him work, even though Grady didn't really know what Will was doing.

After a while Ma came across the field and joined them. The sun was on its way down in the sky and Grady knew it had to be close to supper time. Will was almost done by that time, and all the parts were now put together and back in the pump casing.

Ma didn't say a word. She put her hand on Grady's shoulder and watched with him as Will finished up the job. Will placed the pump back in position, hooked it to the power supply, and turned it on. It kicked in right away. Water flowed through the pump and down the big black hose and into the field. Will smiled real big, and made another of his funny grunting sounds.

Grady laughed. Maybe partly because of the strange sounds

Will made, but partly because he was just so happy to see Will make the broken pump work.

"Dinner is just about ready, men," said Ma. "If you're done here, let's go back to the house."

I am very . . . hung-gree," Will said.

Grady helped gather up the tools. Then Will picked up the toolbox and, without a word, lumbered back toward the barn. Ma and Grady followed behind him.

"He is good with machinery," Ma said. "He must have worked as a mechanic before."

"He could help out a lot around here, couldn't he, Ma?"

Ma gave him a look, but didn't say anything. They walked all the way back across the field without talking and were almost back at the house before she answered. "He can stay with us for now. But don't get too attached to this man, Grady. Some morning you'll get up, and he'll be gone. He doesn't belong here, and he is sure to leave soon."

.9.

Ralwil Turth

One of the most peculiar behaviors of these humans was their love of *games*. Games served no productive purpose that Ralwil could see, yet they were something these humans enjoyed and looked forward to. Grady and Luanne loved to play games, though the Ma didn't usually join them. A few nights after he arrived, Ralwil played a game called *Monopoly* with Grady and Luanne. Ralwil found the whole idea confusing. First they all lay down on the floor around a flat cardboard square. They each picked out a small metal object that was supposed to represent them. Ralwil couldn't decide on an object, so Grady told him to be the shoe. The shoe was interesting, but Ralwil didn't understand how he was like a shoe. Grady was a race car, which reminded Ralwil of his pod, and Luanne was a small dog. Neither of these choices seemed to make sense either.

They each took turns shaking and dropping two small white cubes to determine a random number. Then they moved the piece that represented them the corresponding number of spaces on the cardboard square. When they landed on some squares, they traded colored pieces of paper for colored cardboard cards that matched up with the colors on the square they had landed on. When they landed on some spaces they had to do other things, like pick another card, or move their piece to a different square, or give someone more of the colored pieces of paper. After about an hour, when it was time to go to bed, they had all gone around the board several times, but Ralwil still had no idea what they had done.

A game he liked much better was catch. The first time he played, it was after supper when the sun was down and the sky had turned a purplish gold that reminded him of home. This was his favorite time of the day. Grady gave him a *mitt*, a big bulky thing that fit over his hand. It was a tool in a way, but a type he had never experienced before.

Then Grady ran a distance of about one hundred fornos and turned around to face him.

"You ready?" Grady yelled.

Ralwil didn't know if he was ready or not. He had never played this game before, but he was excited to learn. "Yes," he said.

Grady took a small spherical object, a *ball*, in the hand that wasn't wearing the mitt. He bent forward and looked at Ralwil intently, then contorted his body in a strange dance-like motion, raised the ball over his head, and brought it down very fast, letting it go on the way down. The ball flew through the air in a trajectory aimed directly at Ralwil. The ball got bigger as it came closer. Ralwil's styrpump thumped hard. *The ball was about to hit him!* He stepped aside just in time and the ball flew past his ear. He heard it whistle on the way by. Ralwil turned to watch it land a ways down the yard.

"No, Will! You're supposed to catch it," Grady yelled. "Run down and get it!"

Ralwil turned toward the ball and did his best to run toward it. He was good at walking now, but it was more difficult to move all his body parts faster. If he tried to move too fast, he was sure he would fall down.

He found where the ball had landed, picked it up, and inspected it closely. The surface was white and it was tied together with red fiber. It looked as if it should have been soft, but it felt hard.

"Come on, Will. Come on back and throw it to me."

Ralwil moved back down the yard to the spot he had been before.

"Come on, Will. It's going to be dark soon. Throw it back."

Ralwil gripped the ball with his free hand the way he had seen Grady do, and tried to imitate the dance he did. He swung his arms around, raised the ball over his head, and let go of it on the way down. Ralwil felt a surge of joy as the ball sailed through the air. Grady jumped up with his mitt hand raised high, but the ball was well over his head. It flew right past him. Grady turned around and chased after the ball. He found it and ran back to his previous position.

"Okay," he yelled. He raised the hand with his mitt on it and opened and closed it quickly. "This time, catch the ball."

Ralwil understood now that the object of the game was to capture the ball in the mitt as it sailed through the air. This seemed like a difficult thing to accomplish, but he had accomplished many difficult tasks before, so he was sure he could master this one too. He watched as Grady went through his contortions and launched the ball into the air. The ball shot toward him. Ralwil positioned his body and reached his mitt out to intercept it. The ball flew past his mitt and landed on the far side of the yard again.

Ralwil trotted down to retrieve it. He liked this game. He liked how the ball flew through the air, and how it felt when he wound his arm up and let go of the ball and made it fly. He liked the look on Grady's face when he released the ball, and he liked how it felt interacting with him. He also liked chasing after the ball when it went past him. This game was new, and exciting and . . . *fun*.

Fun was an interesting concept. Ralwil's activities were usually goal directed, focused toward accomplishment of some kind. The idea of doing things just because they felt good was a concept he had never considered before. It felt like a very strange behavior.

Ralwil hurried back to his spot and threw the ball again. This time he got it closer, but it still went over Grady's head. They played on until it was too dark to see the ball anymore. By then Ralwil had captured the ball in his mitt twice, and he'd thrown it close enough for Grady to catch it three times.

"That was fun," Grady said. "Let's do it again tomorrow."

They played nearly every night after that.

.10.

Grady

When they first got out of school, the days weren't long enough. Those first weeks of summer, Grady would finish his chores and then be gone 'til supper time. Some days he'd ride his bike a couple miles down the road to Jerry Clarkson's house and stay there all day, playing ball and just hanging out, talking about things they wanted to do before summer was over. Other days he'd go exploring in the back woods. He'd map them out, or watch bugs on the stump of a tree, or have a water gun fight with Luanne.

A lot of days he'd spend afternoons in the front yard, sitting in the tire swing beneath the big oak tree, reading a book. Early in the summer, there was always something to do and time raced by.

But as the weeks passed, time moved slower and he had to work harder thinking of new things to do. That changed once Will came around. Will made life more interesting. He always had his own way of looking at things, and that made Grady look at things differently too.

The main cash crop on the farm was corn, but Ma had a big garden where she grew green beans, lettuce, potatoes, tomatoes, squash, radishes, and almost all the produce they ate throughout the year. One of Grady's chores was to weed and water the garden every day. Weeding was the most boring thing in the world. He had to bend down and move slowly in between the rows of plants to find all the new little weed shoots that had popped up since the day before. Then he pulled them out of the ground, root and all. After a while his back would hurt, so he'd switch from bending to squatting down. But after squatting a while, his legs hurt too much, so he'd get down on his knees and crawl. This hurt his knees, so he'd switch back to bending over. Up one row, down the next, swatting at bugs, trying to get to the end as fast as he could. He hated the garden. Will loved it.

The first time he helped Grady in the garden, Will leaned over the tomato plants and bent down to stroke a weed with his finger. "This is a weed?"

Grady looked over at a skinny stemmed plant with big broad leaves. "Right," he said. "That's a weed."

He kept on moving down the row. Will stayed by the plant, looking at it closely.

"Why?" Will asked.

Grady stopped his weeding and looked back at Will. "I don't know why. It's just a weed, that's all."

Grady bent down and got back into his rhythm. When he found a weed, he dug it up with his spade and tossed it into a sack around his waist. He'd done this for so long that he had it down to a system, and he could move along pretty fast.

He'd finished one row and was heading down the next, when he looked up and saw that Will was still in the place he had started, and still examining that one weed.

"This is not a weed?" he asked as he pointed to the bushy tomato plant.

"No," Grady said. "That's a tomato plant."

"Why isn't that a weed?"

"Well, that's easy," he said. "People eat tomatoes. They don't eat weeds."

Grady figured that would stop the questions. It seemed like just common sense. He moved on down the row. He didn't want to spend one more second in the garden than he had to.

Will pointed over to another group of plants. "These are weeds?"

"No," said Grady. "Those are squash."

Will looked down at his weed, then over at the squash plants. Grady glanced from one to the other and saw the problem. The weed leaves and the squash leaves looked the same.

"Well," said Grady, "That weed might look like a squash plant too, but it's still a weed."

"Why?" Will asked.

"Well, because we didn't plant it there, I guess." Grady stood up straight and stretched his back and legs. "We planted the squash so they would all be in one place. You can't have squash and tomatoes all mixed together. You have to plant them in rows so they grow right."

He didn't know if Will was satisfied with this answer, but he didn't ask anything else right away, so Grady got back down to work again. Sometimes they had problems getting the vegetables to grow, but new weeds popped up every day. The weeds never have a problem growing, he thought. He concentrated on getting the job done, digging up weeds and plopping them into his bag as quickly as he could. At the end of the row he looked to see where Will was. He was still in the same row but a little further along. He was standing straight up, waiting for Grady.

"Where do you plant the weeds?" he asked.

That seemed like a funny question, but it got Grady thinking. They didn't need to plant weeds because weeds grew like wild all by themselves. Weeds were always around. If they didn't spend so much time stopping them, their whole farm would be nothing but weeds. Why couldn't the plants they wanted grow like weeds grew? If someone made a good plant that grew like a weed, he thought, he could probably make a million dollars. If corn was a weed, you could plant a few seeds of corn and just let them grow. Pretty soon corn would take over the whole field all by itself. Wouldn't that be great. It would sure mean a whole lot less work for them.

They could just sit back and wait for the corn to grow without spending all their time planting and fertilizing and working to get it just right. But if a corn plant was really like a weed, it would start popping up on their lawn and mixing in with other good plants. Then they'd have to find a way to stop the corn from growing where they didn't want it to grow. And if it grew like a weed, maybe it would crowd out all the other good plants they needed. So they would have plenty of corn, but maybe they wouldn't get enough tomatoes. Turning a crop into a weed seemed like a great idea at first, but it could cause a whole bunch of other problems.

He was thinking so much about weeds, that he didn't notice, until he had done a whole row and a half, that he was right in the same row in which Will was standing. Will was bending over a plant, inspecting it closely with an intent look on his face. Grady walked over to see what was so interesting. Will was looking at a beautiful purplish-pink flower. It had grown straight through the leaves of a bean plant and now stood above it, reaching toward the sun. Will leaned in close and smelled it. Grady leaned in too. It had a nice, flowery smell. Just breathing in the aroma made him feel happy. The smell reminded him of his kindergarten teacher, Mrs. Rhodes.

"This is a weed?" Will asked.

Grady thought about it for a second. "I guess it is a weed," he said. "But it's a good weed."

After that he took his time when working in the garden. It still wasn't his favorite chore, but there was always something interesting going on there, when he was open to looking for it.

Grady also liked to visit Will in the barn at night and he would stay out there as late as Ma would let him. After a few days with the family, Ma told Will he could stay in the house if he wanted, but he had made the barn into his own place, and it seemed that he really liked it out there. Out in the barn he had room to spread out. It gave him a place to keep all of the stuff he had accumulated since coming to visit. He'd taken apart and put back together all of their small equipment, and everything worked as good as new, even though there were always extra pieces left over. Will put these extra pieces, and other odds and ends he found, off to the side.

"What's this going to be for, Will?" Grady asked. He sat forward on his tall stool and looked over the workbench.

"Machine," said Will. He picked up a piece from an old car engine and looked at it closely. He turned it over and looked at it just as closely from the new angle. Then he held it next to his ear and listened to it.

"What's the machine for, Will?"

"To go home."

"Oh. Okay," Grady said. He wasn't sure how an invention could help Will go home, and wondered if it would be something like a go-cart. Grady just sat and watched him work. Will wasn't a big talker. He only said what he needed to say. He was a good listener, though.

"Is it going to be an invention, Will? I want to invent something when I grow up," Grady said. "My Dad said I have a good mind for making things. I came up with an idea on how to make a car that turns into a boat. Not the actual invention, but the idea for it. Dad said that was a great idea, but someone had already made it."

Will made one of his happy grunting sounds. He picked up another part and a piece of tubing. He held them together, but they didn't fit. He looked at them thoughtfully for a while before sorting through the other pieces on the workbench. Nothing on the table seemed to be what he was looking for.

"Wait a minute, Will. I have an idea."

They had a whole stack of catalogs off in a corner. Seed catalogs and chemical catalogs, a great big catalog with nothing but tractors and equipment, and all sorts of catalogs filled with tools and hardware. Grady grabbed a bunch and brought them back to the work bench.

"Maybe you can find stuff in here that will help."

Grady flipped through some pages to show Will what was

inside. Will's eyes got large. He pointed to one of the pictures.

"Can get this?"

Grady shrugged. "Sure, I guess. They probably have most of this stuff at the hardware store in town."

"Hardware store," Will said. He nodded his head as he studied the catalogs.

"Hardware store in town."

Will spent a lot of time studying those catalogs after that.

.11.

Ralwil Turth

Hzzzzzzz. Ralwil listened closely. He looked around for the source of the wonderful buzzing sound. Hzzzzzzzz. It was close by and much louder than it should have been, coming from such a tiny creature. Hzzzzzzz. Ralwil loved that sound and how it set his whole ear vibrating. He felt a light touch on his arm and looked down as the *mosquito* landed on him. The insect braced its skinny legs for a good hold before bending its head down and biting into the skin. Ralwil watched closely and giggled with delight. He loved mosquitoes. There were so many exotic creatures on this planet. Chipmunks, birds, and toads were some of his favorites. But of all the fascinating creatures he'd seen, the ones Ralwil found the most interesting were the *bugs*.

Bugs were everywhere. Flying in the air, crawling on the grass, or burrowing into the ground, inside, outside, everywhere. Ralwil loved to observe them. He spent a long afternoon lying on the ground with Grady, watching a parade of ants march by in a long line, carrying bits of leaves above their heads on their way back to their colony. Ants, he felt, had a wonderful civilization, similar in some small ways to his own. Beetles were interesting bugs too. He liked their bright colors and hard shells, and how many different types of beetle there were. Honey bees were wonderful with their furry yellow-and-black bodies. He loved the sound of their buzzing even more than the mosquito sound. He was amazed at how fast flies could move through the air and how far grasshoppers could jump and . . .

Luanne slapped his arm. The mosquito was now nothing but a crushed blob of red.

"I got it for you, Will," she said. "It was about to bite you."

Will looked down at the dead mosquito. He felt sorry for the small creature. That was one of the many oddities of these humans. Bugs were everywhere, but the humans hated the bugs. Not the butterflies or lightening bugs. The human family all liked those bugs.

Bees were looked at as good bugs but were still something to be afraid of. The other bugs were all seen as problems. They swatted at mosquitoes, captured flies on sticky paper, and spent tremendous effort poisoning the bugs that ate the corn in their field. Ralwil felt more and more attached to these humans every day, but these bugs were fascinating creatures too. He wished there was a way these two life forms could appreciate each other.

"Let's play pretend," Luanne said.

It was after dinner and they were outside on the front porch enjoying the cool evening breeze. Grady and Luanne sat on the porch swing. Ralwil sat close by on the front steps.

"No," Grady said. "That's for little kids."

"No, it isn't." Luanne swung her legs back and forth. "Come on, Will. You can play with me."

Will wasn't sure how to play pretend. He didn't know if it required its own game board or something else. "I don't know how to play pretend," he said.

"Yes, you do. You just make believe that you are something that you're not. Then you act that way," Luanne told him.

"It's just a game for little kids, Will," said Grady.

"How about war? You play that with Tom and Billy. That's

pretend."

"Well, that's different," Grady said.

"Or cops and robbers, you play that too."

"We weren't really pretending. We were just playing that way." Grady raised his voice a little.

"We can pretend we're ballerinas." Luanne hopped up from the swing and skipped down the stairs. She raised her arms over her head and brought them together so they pointed at the sky. Then she twirled in circles and jumped around.

"Don't do that, Will." Grady laughed. "You wouldn't make a good ballerina."

Luanne sat back on the grass and laughed too. "No, Will. You wouldn't."

Ralwil wasn't sure what was so funny. He didn't know what a ballerina was, but it looked like a strange thing to be.

"Okay," Grady said. "Guess what I am." He got off the swing and jumped down into the grass. He leapt forward on one leg and landed on the other. Grady kept leaping slowly around from one foot to the other.

"Can't you guess? I'm an astronaut. I'm on the moon."

Luanne did a somersault in the grass, then stood up and

walked unsteadily one way, then the other. "I'm a seasick sailor," she yelled.

Ralwil watched them intently. This pretending was interesting. Luanne and Grady were both moving around in strange ways and acting differently than they usually did.

But they still seemed like Luanne and Grady. Pretending didn't make them different.

Grady stopped leaping around and sat back on the grass.

"Ok. If you could go anywhere in the world, where would you go?"

Luanne rolled over in the grass and stared up at the sky. "I'd go to the North Pole. No . . . maybe Chicago."

"Chicago? You could go anywhere in the world and you'd go to Chicago?"

"Mary Sullivan went there to visit her cousins. She said it was a wonderful place with big buildings and a lake that looks like an ocean. She went to an amusement park with a big roller coaster. I've never ridden on a real roller coaster. I'd like to go to Chicago,"

Ralwil didn't know anything about Chicago or what a roller coaster was, but he wanted to go there too.

"I think I'd go to Australia," Grady said. "I'd live on a beach and have a pet kangaroo."

"No, you wouldn't," said Luanne. "They don't keep kangaroos for pets."

"Maybe not, but it would be great to have a pet kangaroo. How about you, Will? If you could go anywhere in the world, where would you go?"

Ralwil closed his eyes and thought hard. Of all the wonderful places he'd seen or heard about, where would he want to go? He thought of the moon off Wensro in the third quadrant of the AY galaxy. Its crystal mountains, waterfalls, and huge rainbows made it one of the most popular visiting spots in the known universe. He had never been there but had always hoped to see it for himself. The port at Tyrndo-4, where he'd spent a short time while waiting for his next assignment, was a place he'd always wanted to go back to. This port was a major connecting point on the universal trade routes. In a short tour through the market you could see more things than most of his swarm brothers would experience in a series of life times.

There were creatures of every imaginable type, size, and shape, smells of spices and strange foods—some enticing, others repulsive, but all of them interesting—technological marvels, and demonstrations that made him re-imagine what was possible in this life. And the sounds. The air was alive with conversations in tongues he had never heard, music of every sort, and vibrations that made his whole body tingle with delight. But there was one other place he still longed for.

"Home," he said.

After the kids had gone to bed, Ralwil went back to his place in the barn. Luanne was right. He did know how to play pretend. He pretended to be a human and he was so good at pretending, sometimes he thought he *was* a human.

He looked over all the small tubes, engine parts, and plumbing pieces he had laid out on the work bench. Over the short time he had been on this farm, he had learned to love this strange world. But as beautiful as this place was, as intriguing as these humans were, he was here for just one purpose: to fix the power source and leave. He had gotten distracted. He needed to get back to his mission. He picked up a part and thought about how it could help him fix the power source.

.12.

Grady

The family only went in to town once or twice a month, when Ma needed to pick up supplies or meet with people. So the morning Ma announced they would be going to town, Luanne and Grady were excited. They finished their chores in record time, washed up, put on their best school-day clothes, and piled into the car. Usually they argued about who got to sit in the front seat, but that day they both sat in the back because Will came along. They'd never driven anywhere with Will before, and he nearly bounced in his seat with excitement as Ma drove. At first Ma was hesitant about including Will, but he'd been pointing at something in the hardware catalog for the last few nights, insisting that he needed it. At any rate, Ma gave in when it was time for them to go, and Will came along too.

They had an old blue Buick and the air conditioning didn't work, so they drove with the windows open. Grady leaned back in his seat. He loved the feel of the wind hitting his face. The air was filled with the familiar smells of fertilizer and fresh asphalt. It smelled just right for summer. He closed his eyes and listened to the wind, the hum of the engine, and Luanne's nonstop talking. He could tell when they were near town because the car started to slow down.

Glenwood was the county seat, and most of the businesses in the area were located here. They passed the big red brick court-house, the post office, the auto parts store, and the movie theatre, its marquee advertising *Star Wars*. Ma parked on the street in front of Morretti's Market.

Ma shut off the car and turned back to Grady and Luanne. "I just need a few things here. We're not getting any candy today. Okay? Are you two going to be good?"

"Uh-huh. Yes, Ma." They both agreed, though Grady thought her comment was really directed toward Luanne.

They got out of the car and followed Ma into the store. Will walked right behind Grady, looking around like everything was new. Morretti's was a double storefront, and it went back deeper than most of the other stores in town. It was stocked with food and odds and ends of all kinds. A few boxes of produce were at the front, the rest of the store was filled with boxes and canned goods, all stacked in aisles that ran from the front to the back of the store.

As soon as they came through the door, Grady saw Mr. Morretti. He was short and balding, with bushy black eyebrows and a mustache that looked like his eyebrows, only upside down. He always wore a long green apron, and he was usually smiling. He wasn't smiling today, though. He walked over to them, but he looked right past them at Will.

"Can I help you?" he said, in a not entirely friendly manner.

Will looked confused. He didn't say anything.

"It's okay, Mr. Morretti," Ma cut in. "He's with us. This is Will. He's been helping around the farm."

Mr. Morretti nodded, but he still seemed suspicious. "I'm sorry, Mrs. J. I know most of my customers is all." He smiled at Luanne and backed away, but he kept watching Will.

Ma put a few things in her basket as they walked down the aisles. Luanne followed close behind, looking longingly at the treats. Grady hung back with Will. Will stared intently at the shelves. He touched some of the bottles and cans. He picked up a box of Hamburger Helper and stared at the label. Grady thought that was kind of funny, but Ma and Luanne had gotten ahead of them, and Mr. Morretti was standing at the end of the aisle with his arms crossed, so he knew they had to move along. He nudged Will in the ribs.

"Come on," he said. "We need to catch up."

Ma and Luanne were already at the checkout, behind an old lady who was bent over, looking in her purse and counting out pennies. Will watched as the cashier took the last of her money, bagged up her groceries, and wished her a nice day.

Ma stacked the items from her basket up on the counter. The cashier, a teenage girl Grady knew from church, picked up each item, found the price mark, and punched the number into her cash register. She slid the last of the items down to the end of the counter. "That will be ten dollars and seventy-eight cents, Mrs. J."

Ma reached into her purse and counted out a five dollar bill and five singles. Then she dug into the coin section and took out the exact change. Mr. Morretti came over and bagged up the loose groceries, all the time staring at Will. Will didn't even notice. His mouth hung open as he watched Ma give the cashier the money and

Mr. Morretti hand her the bag.

On the way out Mr. Morretti wished them a good day, but it seemed to Grady that he was really happy that Will was leaving. They put the groceries in the car. Then Ma led them all down the street. There were a few people on the sidewalks. Ma nodded to them and said hello as they passed, and they did the same. But Grady could tell that they too were looking at Will, and they didn't seem comfortable. They came to the corner at Gander's Pharmacy. Luanne started to get excited. Gander's had an old soda fountain where they served up double-decker ice cream cones in twelve different flavors.

"Can we stop, Ma? We haven't had ice cream in a long time."

Ma put her hand on Luanne's shoulder. "I'm sorry, Luanne. Not today. Money's tight and I didn't budget for ice cream."

Luanne looked disappointed, but she didn't say anything and she didn't cry, which kind of surprised Grady. They turned the corner to the entrance of the hardware store. Will had been excited before, but now he looked almost ecstatic. Grady wondered what was going on in his head.

.13.

Ralwil Turth

The trip into town was exciting. Ralwil felt anxious at the thought of seeing more of these creatures, these *humans*, in their natural environment. But when they got there, the town was smaller than he expected. From the pictures he had seen on the glowing box, he thought these humans lived in big cities. He expected to see a place teeming with life and buildings of metal and glass that reached up to the sky. Instead, the town was just a few rows of connected buildings, none of them very tall, and though there were people walking around, they were in small groups, not the hordes he expected. Still, he was not too disappointed. What he did see was fascinating and confusing. There was so much to learn about these creatures.

In the market he was amazed at the bright colors on all the food products. Why, he wondered, make each container so strikingly colorful, when a simple description of the food was all that was really needed. And the variety made no sense at all. Almost a whole aisle was taken up by nothing but soup, all in the same red and white cans. The Ma had served soup one night, and he did not care for it at all. It was too runny to stay on his poker, and the more he ate, the hungrier he became. Another confusing thing was something called Hamburger Helper. He had determined earlier that hamburger was a product made from the ground up remains of the long faced stupid animal he had encountered the night he first landed. Hearing that, he felt sorry for the animal and had no desire to taste it. But maybe he misunderstood the situation. As long as he stared at the Hamburger Helper box, he could not understand how it worked. After it had already been ground up, it seemed much too late to help the hamburger.

Another confusing thing was the girl creature taking the items from the Ma's basket and recording their numbers on her machine. Then the Ma handed her some pieces of paper, kind of like the pieces of paper from the Monopoly game. Then they handed the

Ma the products to take with her. When they left the store, he still wasn't sure what had happened. It was some sort of ritual, but it made no sense.

Their next stop was the hardware store. He felt a rush of excitement again as they walked through the doors. Right away he saw several bins of small metallic objects. The place smelled like dust and chemicals, zinc and machine oil. He knew he had come to the right place. Over the last week, he had spent his nights working on a machine to fix the power source. He found some of the items he needed around the farm, and he was doing his best to improvise. But there were several things he could not do without. He walked forward and picked up a small brass object. It was hollow inside, but it had a kind of mechanical shutoff valve built in. That could help.

He was about to put it in his pocket, when he sensed someone standing right behind him. Ralwil turned around. A tall man with bright white hair, thick glasses, and lines criss-crossing every inch of his face, stood next to him. "May I help you?" he asked.

Ralwil was not sure what to say. The people in this town were all so friendly. Everyone wanted to help him. Before he could think of anything to say, the Ma stepped in.

"I'm sorry, Mr. Harris. This is Will. He's helping out around the farm."

"Oh, hello, Mrs. Johnson. I didn't see you at first. How are you? Are you making out all right?"

As they talked, Ralwil slipped away to explore the store. So many interesting things in here. He came to an aisle filled with tubes formed into all sorts of strange shapes. He picked up two of them and, using a connector, fitted them together. That could be useful. He tucked everything under his arm and continued looking. Another bin held spools of wire in all sorts of thicknesses. He took a spool of thick copper wire. He continued to wander around, looking in bins, considering each item. If he thought it would help, he took it. It didn't take long before his arms were loaded. It was hard to carry everything. He cradled his treasures against his chest and headed back toward the front. On the way, he passed a display of large jars. Each jar had a bright red-and-blue picture on the front of a curved pipe. The label read Drain Opener. He wasn't sure he would need it, but it looked interesting. So he grabbed a jar, positioning it between his neck and his shoulder.

When he got to the front of the store, the Ma was still talking quietly with the white-haired man.

"I know we're near the limit," the Ma said. "But if you could just extend us a little more credit, Mr. Harris. As soon as the crop comes in, we'll be able to settle up."

The white-haired man shook his head. "I wish I could, Mrs. Johnson. I really do. But this economy has me stretched, too. I'm afraid that I'm going to need cash up front from now on."

"I don't have the money, but you know we're good for it. You knew my husband his whole life."

The white-haired man shook his head again. "I wish it were that easy, but I can't go any further than I have. I'm sorry."

Ralwil shifted the items he had collected in his arms. It was hard to hold everything. One of the pipes started to slide. He twisted his body to stop it from sliding, but then everything shifted and started to fall. Ralwil felt his breath catch in his throat as all the items he had collected clattered to the floor.

"What's this?" The white-haired man spun around and looked at him sternly.

The Ma put her hand to her forehead and gasped. Grady hurried over from the other side of the store and helped Ralwil pick the items up from the floor.

"Do you have cash for all that?" The white haired man looked down at him with his arms crossed.

Ralwil stood up. His voice came out thick. "Caaash?"

"Money," the man said harshly. "Do you have the money to pay for that?"

The Ma stepped forward. "I'm sorry, Mr. Harris." She put her hand on Ralwil's shoulder. "Let's go, Will."

Ralwil looked back at all the items on the floor as the Ma guided him out the door. In order to fix the power source he needed those items. Why did he have to leave them?

"What's wrong, Ma?" Luanne asked as they moved out to the street.

"Shhhh!" Grady said. "Not now, Luanne."

Ralwil wanted to go back and pick up the parts. Clearly he had done something wrong, but he could think of nothing he had done to make everyone so angry. Then it occurred to him. *Money.* The man asked him for money, and the Ma was saying she had no money now, but she would later. *Money.* The other night after dinner, he had stayed inside the house with Grady and Luanne and watched something on the glowing box. He remembered someone saying how some people had so much money that they could have stuff others couldn't have.

The money was the paper, just like the paper the Ma had used in the ritual at the market. But that made no sense. If the paper was money, it would be easy enough to get more. There was paper all over the place at the farm.

They crossed the street and came to a two story building with tall columns made of a smooth inorganic material in the front. A shiny gold colored plaque was affixed to the side of the building: The Second State Bank of Fulton County. The building seemed different from the others in this town. Not only was it bigger, it seemed more substantial and more important.

The Ma stopped in front of the building and bent down eye level with Grady and Luanne. Her face was red, and her eyes seemed tight. "I need you two to be on your best behavior. No goofing around. All right?"

"Sure, Ma," Grady said.

"Okay, but what's wrong?" said Luanne.

"Nothing's wrong," The Ma turned to Ralwil. "And Will. Will, you need to . . . Just don't do anything, okay? Don't do anything at all."

Ralwil nodded his head. He didn't know what he had done before, but he would try not to do anything now.

They walked inside the building. Now Ralwil was sure this place was important. The ceiling was high in the center, and lights hung down from it. The floor was hard and shiny, and it echoed as they walked on it. A red rope made of some soft looking material hung between two poles and led to a long counter, behind which several women stood in small glass cages. Other people stood in a line by the red rope, waiting to get up near the counter.

He looked at the people in the line. One of them, a fat man in a bright white shirt, held a small bag stuffed with the strips of paper he had seen earlier—the money. He looked at the person at the head of the line, a youngish female, as she handed over one piece of paper. The lady on the other side then handed her several pieces of the money, laying them down in front of her one piece at a time. Suddenly it all made sense. This was some kind of temple to worship the money, and the Ma had come to get some more.

The Ma walked past the line to the far end of the room. A big man, dressed all in blue with a large belly, stood by the edge of the counter with his hands on his hips and watched them as they approached. Ralwil smiled at him, but he did not smile back. At the far end of the room, the Ma stopped by a wooden platform in front of a large glass wall.

Behind it two men were caged behind bigger wooden platforms in separate cubes.

A lady smiled at the Ma. "Good morning, Mrs. Johnson. How can I help you?"

"Hello, Doris." The Ma smiled, but it did not look like her normal smile. "I'm here to see Bruce . . . Mr. McAfferty."

"Yes, of course. One minute. I'll tell him you're here. Please have a seat while you're waiting." She smiled again and walked back into one of the glass cages, where a man sat behind the big wooden platform speaking into some kind of black communication device.

The Ma led them over to a long couch that faced the window, and they all sat down. The lady came back a few seconds later. "Mr. McAfferty will be with you shortly," she said.

Grady sat next to Ralwil, his arms crossed, hardly moving. Luanne sat next to him, swinging her legs back and forth and shaking her whole body.

"Sit still, dear," the Ma said.

Ralwil tried to act like Grady. He crossed his arms and tried not to move his body. It wasn't long before the man got up from behind the platform and came out from his cage. He was tall and thin with a full head of brownish hair. He wore a uniform of sorts, matching gray pants and jacket with thin stripes running down them. A piece of yellow fabric dangled down from his neck. The uniform looked hot and uncomfortable, but Ralwil was sure it had something to do with his high place in the money ritual.

"Helen, how are you? It's good to see you."

The Ma stood up, clutching her purse. "Hello, Bruce."

The man reached into his pocket, then looked at Grady and Luanne. "So how are you two doing? Been helping your mom?"

"Yes, sir," Grady said. Luanne nodded her head.

"Good." The man pulled two long, thin, brown-and-white objects from his pocket and handed one to each of them. "It's okay if they have candy before dinner, isn't it?"

The Ma nodded.

"You're good kids," the man said. "Keep it up. She needs your help." He patted Luanne on the head. His eyes focused on Ralwil, and he hesitated a moment.

"This is Will. He's been helping around the farm some."

"Will, it's a pleasure to meet you." The man flashed his teeth and stuck his hand out.

Ralwil stared at the hand and wondered what the man wanted

from him. After a second, the man lowered his hand and took a step back. "Yes, well." He turned back to the Ma. "Come back to my office, please, Helen."

He took the Ma's elbow and led her back to the glass cage. Ralwil watched as the man sat down behind the big platform. The Ma sat in a chair across from him. Luanne rustled the candy wrapper as she hurriedly opened it.

Ralwil wondered what was happening. The man seemed nice, and this place was surely the place to get more money. But the Ma seemed uncomfortable, like something was not quite right.

"What's wrong with Ma?" Luanne asked.

"Don't talk so loud," Grady whispered back. "You wouldn't understand."

"I would too. Tell me what's wrong? She's not acting right."

Grady sighed. "We don't have enough money, okay?" He spoke softly, but he sounded angry. "We don't have enough money for anything."

"Well, Mr. McAfferty will give her some more then."

"See, I told you that you wouldn't understand. Money doesn't just grow on trees, you know."

From his seat, Ralwil watched the Ma pull a long piece of paper out of her purse. She leaned forward, her hands moving around in the air as she talked. The man picked up some papers, looked at them for a moment, then shook his head. The Ma kept talking, but her body slumped slightly, and Ralwil knew the man was not going to give her the money. They kept talking, but it didn't change anything. Ralwil wished there was some way he could help the Ma.

After a few minutes, the Ma got up from her chair and walked out of the glass cage. The man got up and followed her.

"Helen, please. I hope you'll give careful consideration to my offer. It makes the best of a bad situation."

The Ma's face looked whiter than usual, and her hands were shaking. "All I need is a little more time, Bruce. I thought you would understand."

No one said a word as the Ma led them outside and they walked straight back to the car. Ralwil wished he could help them. The family had been so kind to him. He hated to see them so sad. Nobody talked much on the way home, and dinner time was quieter than usual.

After everyone had eaten and all the dishes were washed and put away, the family gathered around the glowing box. Ralwil stayed in the kitchen. He went over to the counter where the Ma had left her purse. He opened it up and found the place where she kept the paper money. He took out a piece. The paper was colored in green and gray. Looking at it closely, he saw that it had pictures on it. On one side was a picture of a man, on the other was a kind of structure. Both sides had the number twenty set in big type in the corners, and a line of little letters and numbers across it. He took the paper, slipped it into his pocket, and closed the Ma's purse.

Later that night, after everyone had gone to bed, Ralwil went back to his pod. On the way, he picked up a twig from the big oak tree that grew in the front yard. The tree was so tall and its leaves were so full, that when standing under it, he could not see the sky. On hot days it felt nice to stand in its shade. The tree was old and he could feel its strength.

At the pod, Ralwil checked his reserve power. The level was low. He did not want to use any more than he absolutely needed, but the family grouping needed help and he couldn't worry about the power level now. He took out the cellular replicator from his emergency kit, connected it to the reserve power supply, and turned it on. The replicator made nearly identical copies, but there were usually small, random differences in each copy. Ralwil wondered if it would be a problem if the little numbers and letters were not the same on each piece of money. He hoped it wouldn't matter.

The cellular replicator made a low humming sound as the power surged. Ralwil fed the piece of money into the right side of the replicator's intake chamber. He did the same with the twig on the left intake. He fiddled with the controls. An image of the money came up on the right side of the view screen. He hit the magnification button and the picture came in closer. The man's face was drawn with finely etched lines in a complicated swirling pattern. He hit the button again and the image changed. Now he could see beyond the picture, to the fibers that made up the paper and how the ink adhered to it. He hit the button again and the fibers became ropes, huge interlocking strands that wove together in a tangled mess. He hit it one more time, and he was down to the cellular level. He hit another button and the screen split, showing the money cells on one side, and the twig on the other. He went through the same magnification process on the twig, going in deeper and deeper, until the screen showed the double helix of its DNA, the building code of life.

Ralwil took a deep breath, then punched in the finalization sequence. The humming noise grew louder, and the machine glowed. He felt a rush of energy, and the air smelled as fresh as a morning after a thunder shower. The screen brightened. Then, with a sudden zapping sound, the two sides merged into one.

Ralwil reached in and took out the seed of his new creation. This would surely solve all the family's problems.

.14.

Grady

Grady knew Ma was upset when they got back from town. That night she hardly talked at dinner, and when Luanne made a fuss at bedtime about staying up later to watch the next TV show, Ma didn't say a thing. Grady knew they'd had troubles before, and he knew they had to do with money, but this time it was worse. Something had changed. Ma didn't usually let on how she was feeling, but the way she was acting worried him. This wasn't as bad as when Dad died and she'd let the kids see her crying, but Grady could tell this was real bad.

The next morning at breakfast, she wasn't any better. She didn't talk much, and when she did, it was like she barely had the energy to say the words. Grady thought Luanne noticed it too, because she didn't complain about the food and how tired she was, like she usually did. Grady had just finished eating his oatmeal and was cleaning the dish in the sink, when Ma said her first whole sentence of the morning.

"Grady, I think it's about time that Will moved along now. We can't have him staying around here anymore."

"But he's been helping out, Ma. He's done a lot of work for us," Grady protested.

"Well, it doesn't really matter now. It's probably best for all of us." Ma spoke in such a sad way that Grady didn't even think to argue with her. She didn't say anything else after that, and she didn't tell him to get along and take care of his chores, like she usually did. Grady didn't know what had changed, but it didn't take a genius to know it was bad.

Grady felt sorry for Will, but he didn't know what he could do about it. Ma said he was simple-minded. It didn't seem right to put someone like that out on his own. Will had really taken to the farm, and Grady liked having him around. But Ma had made up her mind, and Grady didn't think she was going to change it. Between worrying about Will and Ma and what was going to happen to all of them, Grady felt pretty low. Sticking around the house wasn't helping, so he headed outside.

Grady knew he had chores to do, but Ma hadn't reminded him, and he wasn't in the mood to work anyway. So after he milked Dora and let her out to pasture, he just walked around for a while trying to think of something to do. He could ride his bike down the road to Jerry Clarkson's, but it was hot already, and besides, he didn't want to be around anyone else when he was feeling like this. He could go back by the creek and look for frogs, but he didn't feel like doing that either. He finally decided to go mess around with the ant hill.

The ant hill was up against the foundation at the back of the house, but before he got there, something caught his eye. At the side of their house, between the house and the barn, a small tree was growing. It wasn't big enough to look like a real tree yet, it was more like a shoot, just a couple of feet high and as thin as a reed. But he could still tell it was a tree. In the front yard, near the big oak tree, little trees sprouted up all the time. Grady would cut right over them when he mowed the grass. But it would take forever for one of those little sprouts to grow this big. He wondered how he hadn't noticed it before.

As he got closer though, he noticed that the ground underneath was dug up and piled around its base, like someone had planted the tree.

Dad had planted some trees near the road a few summers before, but no one had planted any since then. Grady couldn't imagine Ma doing this. She had way too much to do just keeping up with regular farming chores and the house and the kids. But he knew it didn't just get there by itself and it made him curious. He kept thinking about it as the day went on.

When he came in at supper time, Luanne was sitting on the stairway with a gloomy look on her face. Grady asked her what was wrong.

"Ma was on the phone today," she said. "She was talking to Aunt Gracie. I think we're going to have to move out there."

Grady made a face. Aunt Gracie was Ma's older sister. She lived in Des Moines and didn't have any kids. She'd married a dentist, and every time they visited, they had to use their quiet voices and take their shoes off at the door. Aunt Gracie wasn't used to having kids around, and Grady didn't think she really liked kids.

"Are you sure? When are we supposed to go?" he asked.

"I don't know. I like it here. I don't want to move to Aunt

Gracie's."

Grady hoped she was wrong, but the way things were going, he was afraid she'd heard it right. Supper was quiet again that night. Grady expected Will to show up like he usually did, but he didn't come by. Grady hadn't seen him around the farm at all since the night they got back from town. So he thought maybe Ma had already told him to leave. It made him sad to think he might never see Will again. After supper they watched TV for a little while. Then everyone went to bed early.

Grady woke up to a crack of thunder that shook the whole house. He stayed up for a while, watching the lightening flash and listening to the rumble of the thunder as the storm rolled over them and then moved on. He didn't know why, but the storm made him feel better. It rained hard for a while. He listened to it drumming on the roof until he fell back to sleep.

The next morning Grady gulped down his breakfast and hurried outside. The rain had stopped, but the ground was wet and the air smelled fresh and rich. The morning was cool, but with so much humidity he knew the heat would be brutal by afternoon. He figured he'd get his chores done early so he wouldn't have to do them later when it got hot.

On his way to the barn he noticed the tree again. The day before it was only at thigh level. Now it was up to his chest, much thicker than before, with several new branches. Grady stared at the tree. Was he seeing this right? Ma grew asparagus in the garden, and there were times where it grew six inches in a single night. One time he'd sat down next to it to see if he could see it grow, but he got bored before he could tell. This seemed like the same kind of thing, only it was a tree, and he'd never heard of a tree growing so fast.

All day long he wondered about that tree. He kept walking past it to see if it had grown any taller. He didn't tell Ma about it, but the mystery took his mind off his other troubles.

That night, Will didn't come by for supper again. Grady was sure that he'd left.

The next morning he went out and checked on the tree before he even had breakfast. It had grown again over the night. Now it was double its size and over his head. Branches sprouted out in every direction, and its trunk was thicker than his waist. He was staring at the tree with his mouth wide open when Luanne came out and stood by him.

Luanne and Grady stared at the tree for a long while without saying a word. Then she touched it, almost as if she was petting it.

"This is a magic tree," she said. " I've been watching it grow and it has to be magic."

"Don't be stupid," Grady said. "There's no such thing as magic."

"Then how did it grow like this? Only a magic tree could grow like this. I think it's a magic tree planted with magic seeds. Just like in Jack and the Beanstalk."

Though Grady told her it was stupid to believe this was magic, he wondered himself. He'd never seen a tree grow like this before, and from what he knew, it didn't seem possible.

Ma sounded a little better at supper that night. She talked about how she'd met Dad and how they took over the farm after Grandpa Johnson died. She talked about how things changed when Luanne and Grady were born, and how much fun they all had together. She told some of their favorite family stories, the funny ones Grady and Luanne always liked to hear. Like the time Ma and Dad won the relay race at the county fair after she twisted her ankle and Dad picked her up and carried her across the finish line, tossed over his shoulders like a sack of potatoes. It felt good to see Ma smile and be happy again. Grady asked her some questions that he already knew the answer to, just to keep her talking. She didn't say a thing about Aunt Gracie.

The next morning he woke up early and ran out to check the tree again. It was twice as big as the day before. Now its trunk was thick enough that he had to stretch to get his hands around it, and he had to bend his neck all the way back to see the top. The bark was thicker and the tree had filled out. The trunk separated about chest high, forming a V, and it branched out from there. Thick limbs broke into thinner branches as it got higher, and it spread out more and more as it reached toward the top so it looked kind of like a pyramid flipped upside down. Grady wondered again if maybe Luanne was right. This wasn't a normal tree. Maybe it was magical. He couldn't think of a better explanation.

For the last few days, Ma had stayed inside most of the time. She kept busy packing things in boxes and organizing all their stuff. Grady and Luanne were sure she was getting ready for the move to Aunt Gracie's. Ma didn't pay any attention to her outside chores, and Grady knew that was going to cause trouble later on. He wanted to tell her about the tree and ask her advice about what to do, but she was too busy to talk, so he just tried to stay out of her way.

The next morning when he went out, the tree was bigger

again. Its top branches reached up above the top of the barn. It looked different that morning. It wasn't until he got real close that he realized why. There were little green buds all over it, from the lowest branches up to the highest. Not just a few—*thousands* of them. Grady looked closely at one of the lower branches. Each bud was part of a cluster of four or five hanging from thin stems that grew out of small bumps in the branch. The bumps were regularly spaced across the branch: top, bottom, and sides. He started counting, but it was hard to keep track of which ones he'd already counted. At any rate, there were a lot. He wondered what was going to happen next. Grady didn't tell Luanne, but he was now convinced of her idea that the tree was magical.

That night, Will showed up at supper time and sat down to eat, just like nothing had happened. Grady couldn't believe Will was there. He was happy to see him, but he wondered where he'd been. Ma didn't exactly seem glad to see him, but she didn't tell him he had to leave either. It felt nice having everybody together again, and Grady went to bed that night feeling better than he had in a long while.

First thing the next morning he checked the tree again. It didn't seem any taller than the day before, and the buds were still there, just like the day before. He felt disappointed. With all that had happened to it in the last few days, he expected more. He didn't know what he thought would be there, but he wanted it to be magical. Grady reached up and pulled one of the buds off the tree. He rubbed between his hands. As he did, he felt it open up and unroll.

He straightened it out and stared at a perfect picture of President Andrew Jackson.

It was a crisp new twenty dollar bill.

.15.

Ralwil Turth

Salmundium. The principle behind the power source was the Salmundium core. Salmundium, the rarest of elements, was mined primarily in the Rhexung-2 galaxy, though trace amounts had been found throughout the known universe. The wonderful thing about the element, and the thing that revolutionized space travel and energy use, was that, when combined under proper conditions with the right organic ingredients, it produced a nearly limitless source of clean-burning power. The process was so simple that every pup learned about it long before he reached his first swarm. Ralwil felt lucky. The power source's malfunction was with the organic composite, not the Salmundium core.

After he had come back from town and fashioned the sprout for the money tree, he knew he had to get serious about fixing the drive. This place was so exotic, and the creatures here so interesting, that he'd been neglecting his own objective—repairing the power source and getting back home. But the reserve power was already low and creating the money tree had drained it further. If he did not come up with a solution to fix the drive soon, he would use up the last of the reserve power. Then it would be too late. He would be stuck on this planet forever.

What could he use to form a new composite? Ralwil began his search in the barn. He went about collecting every organic material he could think of. He took samples of the various chemicals and additives he found in jars and cans on the shelving unit, along with some of the hay they used to feed the cow, and, just in case, some of the cow's dried up waste matter. He picked up some grass and leaves, a handful of dirt, and some oily rags. He also went into the field and collected some of the cornstalks along with a few ears of the immature corn. He wanted to go into the house to look for things there, but it was dark and he knew the family grouping was already in bed.

It might take a while to work through tests on everything, so thinking ahead, after dinner he had filled his pockets with slices of bread, an apple, some cookies, and a handful of cooked corn from the dinner table. Now he had something to eat to keep his energy up while he worked.

Under normal conditions, testing the materials would have been a quick and easy process. But with the power supplies so low, Ralwil had to improvise. The Scurlometer on his omnibelt measured the molecular density and composition of the materials. When combined with a contraption he had designed from odds and ends he found around the farm, he had a crude but effective machine for measuring the materials' usefulness for the composite. His goal was to find something that closely matched the material originally used in the drive. He knew the chances of finding an exact match were nearly impossible. But to cope with emergencies, the power source was designed to run with a wide range of organic materials so that repairs could be made on any planet that contained organic life forms. The trick was finding a material that was a close enough match that it would give the boost needed to jump start the reaction in the Salmundium core.

Ralwil took out the duplicator on his belt and pushed the reset button. He started to laugh as his molecules reformed and the ticklish sensation spread across his body. After a moment, he reformed into his normal shape and appearance. It felt good to be in his own skin again. Using the human creature's body had advantages. After all, he would never have been able to form the bond he had with these humans if he had shown himself in his natural form. The bigger body, with its larger musculature, made it easier to perform the physical tasks around the farm. But it still felt strange walking around in that gawky, cumbersome shell, and he was happy to get back to his real form.

Ralwil collected all his materials and took them into his pod. With the invisi-shield set, he could work inside the pod without any fear of discovery. He set up the equipment and started testing. He decided to test the oily rags first. The process was complicated and time consuming. It took him all morning to set up the first experiment, and when it was done, it showed that oily rags had little-to-no potential use for developing the core. But Ralwil had not expected much on the first try. He cleaned up his equipment and set everything up for the next batch. This time he tested one of the bottles of additive he had found in the barn. The process went more quickly this time, but the results were the same. He kept on working, trying one substance after another, but all with similar disappointing results.

On the second day, his instruments picked up a change in the planet's barometric pressure which indicated a coming thunderstorm. He rigged up a device to draw in the storm's electrical energy and use it to partially recharge his batteries. It felt good being inside his comfortable pod as the storm raged outside, and now he knew that he at least had enough power to finish the testing.

After several days he had gone through nearly all of the materials he had gathered. Though some of them showed some promise, none of them had the potential to provide enough energy to jump start the reaction with the Salmundium.

Ralwil sat down and took a deep breath. He hadn't realized how tired he was. For the first time, he wondered if he would succeed. The power source was designed to work with a variety of materials, but it could not possibly take into account all situations throughout the known galaxy. Maybe the ecosystem on this planet produced native materials that would be only mediocre at best. Maybe it was his fate to be stuck on this planet, hiding in a fake body, forever. While it had seemed exciting at first, lately he was feeling the sharp pains of loneliness. He missed his swarm and wished he were back with others of his kind. Ralwil slumped. He could not remember when he had felt this low.

He stood up, shook his limbs, and moved his body around. He had to stop feeling sorry for himself. That would do no good. Something would work if he kept on trying. It had to. The only way he could fail was if he gave up. Ralwil took another deep breath. Part of his self-pity had to come from working so long without a break. He had been up several days in a row now, working non-stop.

Suddenly he realized how hungry he was. He wished he were back in the big house with the Ma, Grady, and Luanne, eating potatoes. But he did not have any potatoes to eat. He'd already eaten all his bread, the apple, and the cookies. All he had was the corn kernels he had filled his pockets with. He went to where he had left his clothes, reached into his pocket, and pulled out a small handful of the corn. As he did, a few pieces slipped through his fingers and fell on the testing unit of the apparatus. His Scurlometer emitted a low beep.

Ralwil froze. It usually took hours of preparation to get any kind of reading, but if that small an amount set off the meter, maybe there was something promising here. He had already tried the corn from the field—it barely registered. But unlike the hard field corn, this corn was soft, sweet, and tasty. Maybe cooking changed the composition of the corn and made it a better match. He quickly put some more corn on the testing unit and reset the apparatus, then tried to control his excitement as he waited for the results. It took an hour, though it seemed much longer, but when the results came back they were even better than he had expected. Corn might not be the perfect material, but it was the best material he had found yet for the composite.

Ralwil hummed with joy. This was a good first step. He marveled at his good fortune. He needed corn to form his composite, and he had landed right in the middle of a great field of it.

There was still much to do. He had to gather the corn, cook it, and somehow form it into the composite. And he had to do it in a way that would get enough energy in his depleted batteries to initiate the reaction. But he would worry about those things later. For now he just wanted to enjoy his success. He wished he could tell the family grouping of what he had found. He wished he could share with them the news of his good fortune.

.16.

Grady

When Ma first saw the tree, she just stared at it for a long while in shocked silence. Then she pulled a leaf down, unrolled it, and stared some more. She pulled down another leaf and compared it with the first.

"I must be dreaming," she said. "This can't be real."

"It is, Ma," said Grady. "It is real."

"It's magic!" Luanne danced around with excitement.

Ma blinked her eyes.

"This can't be real," Ma said. "But I'm awake, I'm not dreaming. Could this be a miracle?"

Grady thought it might be a miracle too, but he'd never

thought of God doing things like this. In the Bible stories he'd learned in Sunday school, it was always things like parting the Red Sea, or walking on water, or even turning water into wine. This was different. He'd never heard of a tree that grew from a twig to full size in just a week. And he'd certainly never heard of a tree with twenty-dollar bills on it instead of leaves. But he couldn't think of any other explanation, so he figured maybe Ma had it right. Maybe it *was* a miracle.

Ma looked up into the tree and tears welled up in her eyes. She wiped them away with the sleeve of her blouse. Grady looked up into the tree too. The leaves fluttered in the breeze, making a soft rustling sound. His chest puffed up as he felt a wave of emotion wash across his body. They needed money now like never before, and out of nowhere this tree came up and gave them just what they needed. A lot of Bible stories talked about people being tested to see if their faith was strong, and he wondered if they'd been tested too. Tears welled up in his eyes, and Ma reached over and put her arm around him.

Then Luanne stepped up and they all hugged, squeezing tight, holding onto one another like they couldn't let go. Then they were all crying. Tears streamed down Grady's face and it was hard to catch his breath. But he wasn't sad. He felt happy. He didn't think he'd been so happy since before Dad had died. It seemed like the family's luck was changing. After all the bad things that had happened to them, this felt like a new beginning, like things were finally going their way.

Will stood off to the side watching them. Grady looked over at him and smiled. He wondered what Will thought of this whole thing. Will didn't say anything, but Grady could tell he was happy for them. He wondered if maybe Will was the reason things were changing. Their luck had started to get better when he first showed up. Maybe he was their good luck charm? Grady wiped away a tear. He was glad that he had Will back, and he was glad that Ma hadn't sent him away when she said she was going to.

Ma squeezed them tight one more time. Her eyes were red and her cheeks glistened with tears, but she had a big smile on her face.

"Grady," she said. "Will, you too, go get the ladders from the barn. Luanne, come with me. We'll get the bushel baskets."

They set up the ladders at the base of the tree and Grady climbed up to one of the lower hanging branches and pulled one of the leaves. It came off with just a little tug. He passed it down to

Luanne and she put it in one of the baskets. He pulled some more leaves off and handed them down, but just as Luanne placed them in the basket, a gust of wind picked them up and sent them dancing across the grass. Luanne chased after the bills, trying to snatch them as the wind died down, but several got away from her. They skittered across the field, past the barn, toward the creek at the back of their property. After that, Ma sent Will to get some rocks to hold down the bills and keep them from blowing away.

Working together, it took about an hour to fill two baskets most of the way with leaves, each one a crisp new twenty dollar bill. They'd stripped the bottom branches bare, but it hardly mattered. The rest of the tree was still packed with bills. They carried the bushel baskets into the house and stacked the money into neat piles. Ma counted the bills and put rubber bands around each stack. Then she tallied the count on a piece of paper and placed the stacks of bills in a big brown paper grocery sack. When they finished, she was smiling like she used to, a big smile Grady hadn't seen on her face in months.

"Go get cleaned up, kids," she said softly. "We're going into town."

Going into town was always a treat, but that day it was special. On their last trip the week before, they'd left town feeling small. The way Ma's shoulders had slumped down, Grady could tell she felt defeated. This time they went into town like a conquering army.

Their first stop was Gander's Pharmacy, where they walked right past the magazine rack and all the displays of cold medicine and foot powder, straight back to the soda fountain. Ma smiled at the clerk behind the counter, one of the Gander brothers—with their crew cuts, hawk noses, and cold blue eyes, they all looked alike—and reached into her bag for a crisp new twenty dollar bill.

"Four ice cream cones, please. Double scoops."

Luanne beamed.

Grady had a scoop of rainbow sherbet and a scoop of strawberry. Ma and Luanne both had chocolate cones and Will had vanilla. Ice cream always tasted good, but that day it seemed even better. Grady laughed watching Will eat his cone. The ice cream was melting faster than he could eat it, and the melted cream dripped down over his hands and smeared across his face. His eyes were closed. It looked like this was the most wonderful thing he'd ever tasted. They sat on the red vinyl seats and took their time finishing the cones. Some shoppers stared at them. Grady thought it was because of Will. The way he looked, and the way he moved, he surely stuck out in town. For people who didn't know him, he had to seem strange.

After they finished, they made a quick stop at the hardware store where Will picked up the items he'd wanted before and more. Ma paid Mr. Harris for those and for the rest of the money she owed him. He seemed surprised, but he was happy to take the money.

Next they stopped at Morretti's Market where Ma picked up some things for around the house, more groceries, and a lot of sugar for canning and making jams. Luanne asked for candy, and Grady was sure Ma would say no. After all, they'd just had ice cream. But Ma just smiled and said that would be fine. Their cart was loaded when they got up to the checkout line. Grady couldn't remember ever buying as much as they did that day. Mr. Morretti stood off to the side with his arms crossed and a stern look on his face. But when Ma reached into her paper bag and counted out the money, he relaxed. On their way out, he smiled and thanked Ma for her business.

After they'd loaded everything in the car, it was time to go to the bank. Ma gripped her bag tightly and kept her head up and her shoulders straight as they walked across the lobby. Grady had always liked going to the bank. They used to go every Saturday morning when Dad was still alive. Sometimes it was Grady and Luanne, other times Dad just took Grady by himself. They had always stopped and talked with Mr. McAfferty for a while. Then they'd usually go to the diner for a piece of pie, and Dad would drink coffee and talk with the other men gathered there. Grady liked to listen to the men talk. It always made him feel special.

Walking through the lobby that day, Grady thought of Dad and how much he missed him, but also of how proud Dad would be of Ma, Luanne, and him for all they'd done to keep things together through their hard times.

They followed Ma over to the reception desk in front of the big bank offices. The secretary looked up from her typewriter as they came near. "Oh, hello, Mrs. Johnson," she said. "May I help you?"

"Yes, Doris. I'm here to see Mr. McAfferty."

Doris shook her head sadly. "I'm sorry. He's very busy this afternoon. He told me specifically that he doesn't want to be disturbed."

Ma nodded. "I'm sure he is quite busy, Doris. But it's very important that I see him now."

"He specifically said that . . ."

"I understand. But please go get him." Ma spoke softly, and she was still smiling, but there was an edge to her voice that said she wasn't going to take no for an answer.

"Mrs. Johnson . . . "

"Now, please."

Doris hovered over her chair for a moment. Then, without looking Ma in the eye, she walked back to Mr. McAfferty's office. Grady couldn't hear them, but he could see Doris through the glass waving her arms around as she talked. After a second, Mr. McAfferty pushed his chair away from his desk and stood up. As he came out of his office, he was trying to smile, but he didn't look happy.

"Helen, this is a surprise. Have you reconsidered my offer?"

"No, Bruce, I haven't. I've come to pay you what I owe."

Grady almost laughed at Mr. McAfferty's expression. He looked like one of those characters you see in cartoons whose mouth drops open when something surprises them. Clutching her paper bag, Ma walked past him and into his office. Mr. McAfferty followed her and sat down behind his desk. Grady couldn't see everything that happened, but it looked like Ma was taking out the stacks of bills and counting them on his desk. She didn't stay in there long. When she came out, the paper bag was folded flat beneath her arm.

"Let's go, kids, Will. It's time to go home."

They marched triumphantly through the lobby and out the big doors to the street.

The day was beautiful, with big fluffy clouds mostly hiding the sun, and light streaming down in thick yellow rays. It looked like something from a postcard. Grady felt like their luck had changed. They weren't going to have any problems from then on.

.17.

McAfferty

McAfferty sat back in his chair and loosened his tie. Suddenly his office felt hot and his suit felt uncomfortable. He picked up one of the stacks of cash, took off the rubber band, and fanned the bills out with his thumb. He loved new money, and usually it lifted his spirits when he handled it. But now he felt his stomach turn queasy.

This was not the way it was supposed to go. In the twelve years he had managed the bank, he had never seen anyone catch up with their loan payments once they got that far behind. No—that was not true. There was that one fellow a few years back, Garfield, was it? He had borrowed enough from friends and relatives to stop the bank from foreclosing, but within a year he had fallen behind again. McAfferty bought the farm at auction for the value of the note, then sold it off six months later, making a tidy profit on the transaction.

McAfferty had his eye on the Johnson farm for years. It was farm country now, but it would not stay that way forever. All the signs pointed toward suburban expansion, and some day, maybe not for years yet, but sooner than one would think, this whole county would be a mix of big brick homes and smaller aluminum-sided homes. And there would be new roads everywhere, and shopping centers that sold everything from toys to toaster ovens to ladies shoes. McAfferty was a visionary, and he could see the future as clearly as he could see his own hand.

When Sam Johnson died, McAfferty had stepped in right away to console Helen and offer advice. He could help her, if she would only let him. Everyone knew that she was in over her head trying to run the farm by herself. So when she fell behind on her payments, as he knew she would, McAfferty did what he had every right to do. It was legal, and it was fair. He had never imagined that she would come up with the cash to bring her payments up to date.

McAfferty picked up another stack of money and rifled it with his thumb. How did she get the cash? Maybe she had gone down the street to the Mercantile Bank. But if she had, old Charlie Muninger would have called and quizzed him about her loan status. Besides, she would have come in with a check, not this pile of cash. This was most curious.

Where did she get the money?

He fanned through the stack of bills again. This time he sensed that something was not quite right. He brought the bills up to his face and sniffed them. The ink smell was there, but there was something else too. Something familiar, but he could not place what it was. He rubbed the money together. There was something he was missing. Then he touched his fingertips together and he knew.

It was sticky.

.18.

Deputy Schtinkle

Deputy Schtinkle was beginning to hate the Busy Bee Diner. The place itself was not bad. He didn't mind the cracked red vinyl seats and faded Formica counters. Its food was moderately priced, the coffee always fresh, and the service reasonably friendly. Plus, it was located in the middle of the downtown business district, right across from city hall and the Sheriff's office, and this was the place to hear all the local buzz.

He had actually liked the diner back when he just stopped in once in a while for a cup of coffee or a quick lunch. But now the sheriff had taken an interest in him and insisted that he sit with him in the diner. So he did, hour after hour, day after day. Doing nothing, when he could have been out on the street, fighting crime. Deputy Schtinkle was really starting to hate this diner.

With the lunch rush over, the crowd had thinned out. There were only a few people left. A couple of farmers sat up at the counter with their seed caps on, talking about the weather. At a table in the middle of the room, three elderly businessmen finished their lunch while hardly exchanging a word at all. And up front by the window, wedged into his customary booth, Sheriff Reynolds sat where he had a good view of the outside door and his office across the street. Deputy Harold Schtinkle sat across from him, like he did every afternoon at this time, drinking way too much coffee and wishing he was somewhere else.

Today Al Freely, the Chevy dealer, had pulled up a chair and joined them at their table. Freely was short and balding and he always talked too loud. He wore a blue-and-green checkered sports jacket and a bright red-and-yellow tie with a big grease splotch right in the middle of it. Freely always dressed in loud colors. If his clothes could talk, they would surely scream *Look at me!* He had finished his lunch and just started on a big piece of flaky-crusted cherry pie. He cut a piece with his fork and stuffed it in his mouth. He kept on talking with his mouth full. "You really need to . . .

mmphmm."

"What?"

Freely swallowed and washed the pie down with a swig of milk. "I tell you, Sheriff, you really need to replace those patrol cars. Just give me the word and I can get you a great deal on some brand new ones."

"Can't do it. It's not in the budget." The sheriff crossed his arms and looked out the window.

Deputy Schtinkle tried not to smile. The sheriff had been on a new diet for the last two weeks. He had just finished his lunch of a plain hamburger patty, cottage cheese, and a side of peaches—the same lunch he'd had for the last two weeks straight. Normally the sheriff was good-natured and easy-going. Lately he had become increasingly grumpy. Freely was usually just a small annoyance, but now, watching him eat that pie in front of him had to be torture.

"Well, maybe not new then. But you won't believe the deal I can get you on some good used vehicles."

The sheriff shook his head and continued to stare out the window. They'd had this same conversation just the week before. Deputy Schtinkle looked over at the sheriff and wondered if that was what he was going to become, a fat gray-haired has-been Sheriff who was more concerned with his next meal than with keeping the public safe. Schtinkle was young now. He had just turned twenty-five, and he was pencil thin with a full head of dark brown hair. Recently he had grown a mustache which, he thought, made him look burly and tough, though no one seemed to notice. The way things were going, he could see the future, and it was sitting right across from him.

Since he'd been a boy, he had always wanted to be a policeman. All his favorite movies and TV shows were about policeman and detectives. They were the heroes, risking danger to catch the bad guys and bring them to justice. It was all so exciting on TV. But nothing exciting ever happened around here. Nothing.

"Or how about for yourself, Sheriff? Maybe you or the Mrs. could use a new car?" Freely cut off a second bite of pie and popped it into his mouth.

The sheriff kept staring out the window. "Look over there." He pointed out at the sidewalk. "It looks like McAfferty is on his way over. The way he's rushing, you'd think someone was behind on his payments or something."

Freely glanced out the window with a look of alarm, quickly looked at his watch, and stood up. "My gosh. Look at the time. I didn't realize how late it was."

He dropped his fork on the plate, threw some money on the table to pay for his lunch, and hurried out the side door of the restaurant, leaving his pie behind.

No sooner was he gone than Bruce McAfferty came in the front door. His face was slick with sweat. Schtinkle wondered why he insisted on wearing that heavy suit in this hot weather. Who was he trying to impress? No one else in town wore a suit.

McAfferty came straight to their table and, without being invited, sat down in the seat that Freely had just abandoned. "We've got a big problem here, Sheriff."

The sheriff took a long sip of his coffee and eyed the discarded pie. "Is that so?" he asked.

"Darn right, it's so. Helen Johnson just came into my office and paid up her entire past due balance. Just like that."

"Did she now? Well, good for her." The sheriff licked his lips as he stared at the pie.

Deputy Schtinkle wondered if the sheriff would pick up his fork and take a bite. Schtinkle bet he would. Two weeks on a diet was as long as the sheriff ever lasted, and Schtinkle had been wondering how long it would be before he broke down this time.

"That woman's had more than her share of problems with Sam dying and all, and trying to take care of the farm and those young kids," the sheriff went on. "It's about time she caught a break."

Deputy Schtinkle was starting to drift off. He wondered what he was going to do this weekend. Maybe he'd check out that fishing hole that Jerry from the filling station had told him about. It wouldn't exactly be exciting, but at least it would be something different.

"No, that's not it. She came in and paid it off with cash. She had a grocery bag stuffed with money—all brand-new twenty dollar bills."

Suddenly the conversation caught Schtinkle's attention. A grocery bag of cash?

Had he heard that right? This sounded interesting.

"Well, maybe she came into an inheritance." The sheriff glanced up and took another sip of his coffee, but his eye strayed back to the pie. "Or maybe some life insurance paid out."

"No, no. It's nothing like that. I've already checked, and there's no way she could have gotten that much cash."

The sheriff shrugged. "So maybe they had some money

around the house, or she won the Irish Sweepstakes, or who knows where it could have come from, Bruce. There's no crime in having cash. Not that I know of anyhow."

"Something's wrong here." McAfferty reached into his front shirt pocket and took out a crisp new twenty dollar bill. "Here, take a look at this." He handed it over to the sheriff.

The sheriff reluctantly took it and looked it over closely, first the front, then the back. "So what's wrong? It's a twenty dollar bill. It looks fine to me."

"Can't you tell? It's sticky!"

The sheriff looked at the bill again. Then he rubbed it with his fingers. "Maybe it is," he said. "Not noticeably though." He handed back the bill. "What are you saying, Bruce? Are you saying that Helen Johnson is involved in something fishy?"

"Maybe."

"Helen Johnson? Come on, Bruce." The sheriff shook his head. "That's the craziest thing I've ever heard."

McAfferty pushed the pie plate away from him and put his elbows up on the table.

"Well, what about that stranger that's hanging around their place now. What about him? There's something peculiar about that man."

A stranger? Deputy Schtinkle leaned forward with interest. This was getting better.

The sheriff looked down at the pie, which was now nearly in front of him. Schtinkle could tell his will power was melting. It was only a matter of time now before he picked up the fork and took a bite.

"A stranger?" the sheriff asked. "Are you talking about that farmhand who's helping around her place? She called me and I checked that out weeks ago." He picked up his fork and jabbed the air for emphasis. "How do you expect her to run a place that size without help?"

McAfferty didn't say anything right away, and Schtinkle thought that was going to be the end of the conversation. But just then the group of elderly businessmen at the table in the middle of the room got up and started shuffling toward the cash register. One of them, old Mr. Harris from the hardware store, broke from the group and made a bee line for their table.

"Are you talking about Helen Johnson?" he asked.

McAfferty looked up and nodded his head. "That's right. We are."

"Well, the strangest thing happened today. She's been behind on her bill for months. I felt sorry for the poor woman, and I always wished her the best and did whatever I could to help her, but after a while . . . you can only go so far. Business is business, right?"

McAfferty nodded. "That's right."

"But then today," Harris went on, "she came in and paid off her whole balance with fresh new twenty dollar bills. I've never seen anything like it."

"See!" McAfferty wagged his finger at the sheriff. "See what I'm talking about?"

Harris kept talking. "And that big farmhand she's with scares me. You know, I'm as open minded as anyone, but he's different from folks around here. I don't know what it is, but something's not right about that fellow."

McAfferty nodded his head enthusiastically. "That's right. That's what I said too."

Schtinkle tried to contain his excitement. This kept getting more interesting.

"I don't know . . . " The sheriff looked like he had just stepped in dog doo. Schtinkle could tell he still didn't want to get involved. The sheriff put his hand to his chin like he always did when he was thinking. Without seeming to realize what he was doing, he cut off a big bite of cherry pie and stuffed it in his mouth. He chewed noisily. "I don't know."

Schtinkle tried to hide his smile. He knew the sheriff was going to eat that pie. He paid attention. He looked at things and people closely. He noticed things others missed. That was why he was going to be such a great detective. He cleared his throat loudly and announced, "I'll do it."

The three others looked at him like they were noticing him for the first time.

"Leave it to me. I'll look into it," Schtinkle said. He felt a buzz of adrenaline surge through his body. This was the big chance he had been waiting for.

.19.

Grady

Grady thought how funny it was that a person could feel as low as dirt one day and be on top of the world the next. That's how he felt after they found the money tree. He knew that money can't buy happiness, but everything sure was going their way now. He started thinking about all the stuff they could buy, now that they were rich. The first thing he thought of was a new bike. He had an old bike that worked fine, but it only had three speeds, and the paint was dull, not like the shiny new bikes some of his friends at school had. Then he thought maybe they could get a pinball game like the one in the back of the pizza parlor in town. He could have it fixed so he didn't have to put in quarters, and he'd keep it in his room where he could play it any time he wanted. Luanne talked about getting a new doll house for her Barbies, a big one with extra rooms and all the accessories. To Grady it felt like the times before Christmas, when he and Luanne flipped through the big Sears catalog and made up lists of everything they wanted, only now they really had the money to buy some of it.

Ma told them not to get carried away. She said the tree was a gift, and they needed to use it wisely. They shouldn't tell anyone else about it either, she told them. This was a strange and wonderful gift, but people wouldn't understand. Some people would be happy for them. Others wouldn't, and some would even wish them ill.

None of that made much sense to Grady. This was something so amazing that he wanted to tell everyone he knew. He wanted to have people come over so he could show them the tree, and they'd see what a great thing they had. It was confusing. Ma always told them not to keep secrets, but now she was telling them that they couldn't tell anyone about what had to be the best thing that had ever happened to them. Grady didn't understand any of it at the time, but after they went to church on Sunday, he started to see what she meant.

They belonged to the Congregational Church in town, though

they hadn't been there much over the last few months. Back before Dad died, they'd gone every Sunday. Dad was an usher and he always greeted everyone at the door with a handshake and a smile. Back then, going to church was as natural as going to school.

After Dad died, they went for a while, but it felt different. Ma never said it right out, but Grady thought she felt uncomfortable being there. She knew that people felt sorry for them, and she didn't want their pity. They gradually started going less and less. Ma said that what was in their hearts every day was more important than what happened in some building on Sundays.

On Sunday, Ma woke everyone up early, fixed a big breakfast, and told Grady and Luanne to put on their best Sunday clothes. Will came with them too. Ma gave him one of Dad's old suits to wear, and he looked different dressed up like that. The suit was tight, and Will kept tugging at his collar. But Grady had to admit, he looked distinguished, like he was someone important. Right before they left, Ma went to the money tree and pulled down a couple of leaves to put in the collection plate.

They pulled into the parking lot just as the church bell started ringing. They followed an elderly couple inside and sat in the last pew. Mrs. Martin turned around from the pew in front of them, smiled, and, in a voice big enough to be heard all the way up front, said hello to Ma and how glad she was to see her back in church again. Ma smiled back at her, but she didn't say a thing.

Luanne waved to a girl a few rows over. She'd been excited about going back to church. In the car she'd talked about how much she liked Sunday School and how she hadn't seen some of her friends since school got out. Grady saw Charlie Taylor, a kid from his class, and nodded at him. He nodded back. Several people turned their heads, stealing a quick glance at Will. Grady didn't think much of it. The same thing had happened when they'd gone into town. It seemed kind of rude, but he guessed Will was used to it. Then the organist began to play and everyone pulled out their hymnals and started to sing.

The song was "Onward Christian Soldiers," one of Grady's favorites. He was following the words in the book and singing along with the congregation. They were well into the second verse when Will started to sing. Grady was enjoying the song and didn't notice it at first. But after a minute, when a lot of the other voices stopped, it was hard *not* to notice. It wasn't that Will had a bad voice, but he was loud, and he sang in a way all his own—a deep croaking sound, like a fog horn, only with more enthusiasm.

Grady stopped singing and looked up at Will. About half the people in the church were looking at Will too. Luanne was laughing, and though Grady didn't look at her, he was sure Ma was turning red. Will went on for another line. Then Grady dug his elbow into Will's side until Will looked down at him and stopped singing. Then the rest of the congregation picked up again and tried to go on like before.

Will looked down at Grady, puzzled.

"Not so loud." Grady whispered up at him, "You need to sing softer."

Will still looked puzzled, but he sang more quietly after that.

The pastor talked some then, and they sang another song. Will did what he was supposed to, standing up when everyone stood up, and sitting down when everyone sat back down. The pastor preached his sermon, something about how Christian love conquered all, but Grady wasn't really paying attention. He was thinking about how hot it was in the church, and how he wished they could open some windows. Then he started thinking about the windows here, which were all made of stained glass, and some of them looked pretty interesting. The stained glass pictures showed scenes from the Bible. With their bright colors and the way they were divided into panels, the windows looked almost like a comic book. Then he started wondering what would happen if they'd had superheroes back in Bible times, and before he knew it, the pastor had finished with his sermon and everyone was standing up and singing again.

Then the ushers passed around the collection plate. When it got to the family, Ma pulled the leaves she'd picked from her purse and placed them in the basket. Mrs. Martin pretended she was getting something out of her purse too, but from the way she was turned, Grady knew she was looking back to see what Ma gave. He noticed a few others look over too. Then the ushers collected the baskets and marched up front to the altar while the organist played another song. After that, it wasn't long before the service was over. Grady and Luanne went off to Sunday school, while Ma and Will met with the other grownups for coffee in the big meeting room.

During the school year, Sunday School was divided by age groups. In the summertime, not as many people came to church, so all the kids met together in one class, where they sat together in a big circle. Their teacher, Mrs. Dirking, was a fat lady who always smiled and smelled like talcum powder. She'd been talking about Joshua and the walls of Jericho. When she went to the blackboard to draw a picture, Mindy Adams, who was a year older than Luanne, whispered something in her ear. Luanne got this look on her face and shook her head. Then she whispered something back to Mindy. Mindy whispered something back to her. Then Luanne suddenly started crying.

Mrs. Dirking turned from the blackboard. "Luanne, what's the matter?"

Luanne shook her head and didn't say anything. She gasped for breath and her body shook with her sobs. Luanne cried sometimes at home, but never out in public where other people could see her. Grady wanted to go over and give her a hug and tell her it was all right. But he didn't want to call attention to himself either, so he stayed in his seat and didn't say a thing.

Mrs. Dirking gave a big sigh, then walked over and put her hand on Luanne's shoulder. "Come on, honey. What's wrong?"

Luanne shook her head and started crying even harder. Grady could tell that Mrs. Dirking didn't know what to do. Mindy Adams had this smug look on her face. Grady wondered what she'd said to make Luanne cry. He wanted to yell at her, and tell her it was a sin to be mean in church. But at the same time, he felt kind of embarrassed that Luanne was acting like this. So he stayed in his seat and didn't make a sound.

After another minute or so, Luanne wasn't getting any better, so Mrs. Dirking turned to Grady with a pleading look and said, "Grady, honey, can you take your sister outside, please?"

Grady was happy to get up. He nearly jumped out of his chair. He took Luanne's elbow, pulled her up, and guided her out the door. He stopped in the hallway and gave her a tight hug. "What happened?" he asked.

She kept sobbing, but she tried to talk. "She . . . she . . . she said wc stole the money!"

Grady clenched his fists. He thought about going back into the room and telling Mindy Smith off, but instead he just squeezed Luanne a little tighter.

"She said her parents were talking and . . . and they said we must have stole the money, 'cause there's no other way we could have got it, and I told her we didn't, but she said if we didn't steal it, where did we get it? And I couldn't tell her!" Luanne broke into another round of sobbing.

"Let's go," Grady said. "Let's go outside."

Grady put his arm around her shoulder and they walked down the hallway, past the big meeting room where all the adults were talking. The air smelled like fresh coffee and buzzed with conversation. Grady thought about going in and looking for Ma, but he decided not to bother her.

They walked down the hall and out the big double doors at the front of the church. Outside the sunshine hurt his eyes, but the air smelled clean and fresh. Ma was already outside, standing at the edge of the sidewalk with Will. Her arms were crossed and she had a distant look on her face. Grady was surprised to see her out here. He wondered if Will had done something goofy again.

Ma saw them and ran toward them with concern on her face. "Luanne, Grady!

What happened?"

Luanne wiped her tears on her sleeve and shook her head. "No . . . nothing," she said.

Ma looked at her, but she didn't pursue it.

On the way home, nobody talked much. It seemed to Grady like they wouldn't be going back to church again for a while.

.20.

Deputy Schtinkle

Dressed head to toe in the camouflage outfit he had bought from the ad in *Soldier of Fortune* magazine, Deputy Schtinkle knew he was as close to invisible as a man could be. He slunk down as close to the ground as he could, quickly ran ten steps forward, and hid behind the cover of a small tree. He took a deep breath, then reached down to the binoculars that hung from his neck and brought them up to his eyes. He adjusted the focus and scanned the area. No one was there and nothing was happening. He sighed and let the binoculars drop back on their strap. He'd been watching the farm for nearly four hours, and so far he hadn't seen even one sign of suspicious activity. This was starting to get frustrating.

The sheriff had told him that the whole idea of running an investigation of Helen Johnson was ridiculous, and he would have nothing to do with it. This meant that Deputy Schtinkle had to pursue the case after hours, on his own time. It took longer to get things done this way.

He had spent the next two days around town, interviewing people who knew Helen Johnson and her family. Some people, like the old school teacher with all the cats, had only nice things to say about her. But he pieced the whole story together after talking with the downtown merchants. It seemed that she'd had no money to speak of before.

Now, suddenly, she was loaded. She must have gotten the money from somewhere, and as far as Schtinkle was concerned, it had to be from somewhere illegal. Something was rotten here, and he was going to find out what it was.

He had to take care of his normal duties first, so he was not able to get out to the farm until late afternoon. He parked his cruiser on Schmidt Road, down a ways from the Benders' farmhouse. He planned to hike along the creek behind the Johnson farm. On the map it all looked pretty straightforward, but he took a wrong turn and wandered around in a corn field for close to an hour before he finally found the creek and followed it to where he could see the big barn. Then he settled in and waited for something to happen.

But nothing did. He raised the binoculars and scanned the area again. Still nothing.

Maybe he was too far back. He wished he had spent the extra money to get high magnification binoculars, but on his salary he could only afford so much. He glanced at his watch. It was getting late. He needed to quit his surveillance soon, or he'd never find his way back in the dark.

He was just about to call it off for the night, when suddenly he saw movement. He raised his glasses and focused. The view was blurry, but he could tell it was a person, and as big as he was, and with a bald head and all, this had to be the farmhand, the one he had heard so much about. His heart thumped with anticipation. This was it. Now he would see some action. Now maybe he'd find out what was happening on this farm. He watched as the big man made his way from the house to the barn and went inside.

Deputy Schtinkle leaned forward and waited for him to come out. After a few minutes, with no sign of the farmhand reappearing, Schtinkle couldn't control his curiosity. What was the man doing in the barn? For all he knew, the man could be running a printing press, churning out counterfeit bills in there. Or maybe he was part of some drug ring and was using this farm as a cover for his evil schemes. Or maybe they were all communist spies, and this was part of some ingenious plan to take over the country. He knew it was possible because he once saw a story just like that on TV. The farmhand could be doing just about anything in that barn, and Deputy Schtinkle would not know a thing about it. He started to sweat. It had to be something bad. And sitting back here, so far away, he was helpless to stop it.

He had planned to watch from a distance, but how could he sit back here when something awful could be going on? What kind of detective would he be if he just watched and didn't lift a finger to stop it? He had to move in closer.

He was about fifteen yards from the creek, well hidden in an overgrown wild area with tall grasses, thick bushes, and some small trees. The trick was to get across the creek and up to the barn without being seen. Schtinkle took a deep breath, crouched down, and started running forward. He had only gone a few feet when he stepped in a hole and his foot got stuck. *Drat!* His foot did not hurt, and it didn't feel like he'd twisted anything, but he felt his foot wedge in tighter as he tried to pull it out. He stopped for a second to think this through. It was probably just some gopher hole. But what if it was a booby trap? With the activities this Johnson gang was involved in, it would make sense that they had taken precautions. He would have to be more careful moving forward. He pulled his leg as hard as he could. Suddenly, with a popping sound, his foot came free. He sighed with relief. Then he realized his shoe had stayed in the hole. *Drat!* He reached down into the hole, but his shoe was wedged in so tightly he couldn't even move it. Deputy Schtinkle sighed. He'd need a shovel to dig the shoe out, and he hadn't thought to bring one. He'd have to come back and get it later. He hoped he would remember the spot where he'd lost it, but for now he had more important things to do.

He moved forward again. It felt awkward creeping forward with one shoe on and one foot in just a bare sock, but he had no other choice. A little further on, the tall grasses changed to a thick wall of bushes. He could walk around them, but that would take him longer. And knowing the Johnson gang, they'd probably planted more booby traps at all the places that would be easier to get through. Well, he was too smart to fall for that. He got down on his belly and started to crawl through the bushes.

He was only a few feet in when he felt something scrape his

arm. *Darn, that hurt!* He wiggled a little farther and he felt another scrape against his cheek. That was when he realized he was going through a wall of thorn bushes. He tried to turn his head to see how he could get back out, but he got scraped again. *OW! That one really hurt.* He was already in too far to give up. He gritted his teeth and kept crawling forward. *Ow!* Now every time he moved, he felt another thorn dig into his flesh. They cut through his clothes and stung against his skin. He kept moving, every inch more painful than the last. *Ow!*

Finally he got through to the other side and pulled himself all the way out. He was at the top of a small hill, right next to the creek. He stood up and brushed off the dirt. His shirt and pants were tattered and his arms were streaked with long red scratch marks. He couldn't see his face, but based on how it felt, he knew it wasn't pretty. At least he had made it through. Now to get across the creek and on to the barn. The sun was down and it was getting dark. He had no time to spare. Deputy Schtinkle crouched down and took a step forward, but his sock slipped on some loose dirt and he tumbled forward into the creek, landing with a splash. He quickly stood up, gasping for breath and shivering. The water wasn't cold, but he was soaked completely through.

This hadn't gone at all like he had planned. He bent down and fished his binoculars out of the creek. Maybe he needed to rethink this whole idea. Maybe he was going about this the wrong way. In fact, maybe the whole idea was wrong. The sheriff had insisted that Helen Johnson would never do anything illegal, and most of the town's people he'd talked with said the same. Even the merchants spoke highly of her, though they could not understand where the money had come from.

The more he thought about it, the clearer it became that he was wasting his time. He could be home right now, watching detective shows on TV, instead of standing here, soaked like a wet rat. He stepped out of the creek and onto the bank. His sock made a sucking sound as he did. What was he thinking, running off on a wild goose chase like this?

As he started to climb up the bank, he saw something in the bushes he had just crawled through. It was getting darker and it was hard to see clearly, but it looked like something was stuck in there. Curious, he moved closer. Yes, there was definitely something. In fact, it looked like three separate somethings. He wished he had thought to bring a flashlight with him. He came to the bush and reached, ignoring the pain as a thorn bit into his hand again.

He grabbed onto the object and pulled it out. It felt like paper. He pulled it up close to where he could see it better. His heart nearly skipped a beat.

It was a crisp, new, twenty dollar bill.

.21.

McAfferty

When he came into the bank that morning, McAfferty was surprised to see a light on in his office. On a normal day, the assistant manager would open up the bank, all the tellers would get in early to set up their drawers, and Doris would be in position at her desk, right where she was supposed to be. He would come into the bank two minutes before the doors officially opened and do a quick walk-through, just to make sure everyone was on their toes. Then he would go into his office, open the curtains so he could keep track of what was going on out on the floor, and get to work.

But if his lights were on, that meant someone was already in his office, and that made no sense at all. He skipped the inspection and walked straight back toward his office.

Doris got up from her desk as he came closer, a worried look on her face. "I'm sorry, Mr. McAfferty. He was waiting by the front door when Mr. Schiller opened up. He insisted on waiting for you in your office."

McAfferty felt a flash of irritation. It was bad enough that someone came by first thing in the morning without an appointment, but the fact that Doris had let someone in his office, before he even had a chance to set up for the day, that really irritated him. McAfferty hardly paused as he walked past her. "Get my coffee, Doris."

He was at his office door before he realized that he didn't even know who was inside. He thought of calling back to Doris to ask who was there, but he thought better of it. It didn't matter who was inside. This was *his* office, and nobody else belonged there. He would sure enough give the intruder a piece of his mind. He straightened his tie and checked his posture, then opened the door.

Before he was even inside, he noticed the damp, ripe smell of dirty laundry. He wrinkled his nose and hoped he wouldn't need to get his chair cleaned. Then he stepped all the way in and looked at the man sitting in the chair across from his desk. At first he didn't recognize him. His hair was matted down, his eyes were bloodshot, and he had little burrs stuck in his mustache. His face and arms were covered with scratches, and he was half covered in mud. This man was a mess. Now it really steamed him that Doris had let the man come in to wait in his office. He was about to bark at the man to get out and call back if he wanted an appointment, when he realized who the man was. It was the deputy, the one who hardly talked. What was his name? And why did he look like that?

"What happened to you?" he asked.

"I got caught in a thorn bush, then I fell into a creek, and on the way back I got lost in a cornfield, and . . . "

"Never mind." McAfferty noticed the man was wearing only one shoe.

Unbelievable. He walked behind his desk, sat down, and pushed the intercom button.

"Doris? Where's that coffee?" McAfferty leaned back in his chair. His world was supposed to be well organized and orderly. He hated surprises. He hoped that this was not an indication of what the rest of his day would be like. "Okay, what do you want?"

The deputy was about to speak when there was a short knock on the door and Doris walked in with a steaming cup of coffee.

McAfferty held his hand up for the man to hold on. He waited as Doris set the cup down on the edge of his desk and quickly retreated from the room. McAfferty picked up the coffee and took a small sip. At least the coffee was good. He put it back down and motioned to the deputy. "Go on."

The deputy did not say a word. Instead he reached into his pocket and pulled out three damp, crumpled, twenty dollar bills. He reached across the desk and handed them to McAfferty.

McAfferty took them reluctantly. He smoothed them out and let them drop on the desk. His nose wrinkled again. He hated dirty money, and wet dirty money was the worst. "Look, Deputy . . . "

What was his name? He had no clue. "If you want to open an account, they can help you up front. Now I'm quite busy and . . . "

"No, sir. You don't understand. I found this over by the farm. The Johnson farm."

McAfferty sat up in his chair. Now this was interesting. He picked the bills up again and looked them over carefully. "Tell me about it," he said.

"Well," the deputy said, "I put the Johnson farm under surveillance around four thirty-seven yesterday afternoon, and . . . "

McAfferty shook his head. "No, I don't have time for the

details. What happened?"

The deputy looked disappointed. "I was at the back of the farm, by the creek where it's all wild, and I found this money in some bushes."

McAfferty sat back and let that sink in. Could it be a coincidence? Was it possible that someone had just dropped the money and the wind had carried it away? Or was so much cash going through the Johnson farm that they couldn't keep track of it all? Out in the middle of the country like they were, it wasn't likely that someone had just lost the money and it happened to blow into their bushes. One twenty dollar bill would be a coincidence. Two maybe, though that tested the limits of believability. But three? Three twenties surely meant that something was going on.

"So?" he asked. "How did they get there?"

The deputy shrugged his shoulders. "I . . . I don't know."

"Did you notice anything out of the ordinary? Anything suspicious?" McAfferty picked up the wet bills and ran his fingers along the edges.

The deputy shook his head and looked down at the floor. "No. Not really."

McAfferty looked at the bills again. These were just like the others that Helen Johnson brought in. They looked good and felt good. If they were counterfeit, they were flawless. But something was fishy about this situation. He looked back at the deputy.

"What do you think is going on, Deputy?"

The deputy sat up straight in his chair and nodded his head. "Well, I do have some theories." He stroked his mustache and pulled out a burr. "It could be an organized drug operation, or I'm thinking they could be spies . . . "

"Spies?"

"They could be."

McAfferty shook his head. This was ridiculous. *Spies?* Something was going on at the farm, but he didn't think spies were involved. In fact he couldn't imagine Helen Johnson doing anything unethical, let alone illegal. Still, something strange was going on. The whole town was buzzing with talk of how Helen suddenly had money to spend. And based on this deputy's story, it sounded like there was so much cash on the farm that money was just lying on the ground out there. McAfferty lifted the bills near his face and sniffed them. They were wet, but they still smelled like money. He laid the cash back down on his desk. *Where was all this money coming from?* He had to know, even if it meant dealing with this ridiculous deputy.

"Okay, it looks like you might be on to something," said McAfferty. "But why are you telling me, and not the sheriff? What do you get out of this?"

The deputy puffed out his chest. "Well, it's not like I've thought of it before, but there is something. The sheriff, you know, he's a good sheriff, but he is getting old."

McAfferty picked up the money again as he waited for him to go on.

"And he is getting old, so it's well . . . you know."

"What? You want to be sheriff?"

"Well, I hadn't really thought of it like that before, but now that you mention it, a change might be a good thing."

McAfferty nodded. "And you think I can help you?"

The deputy looked down at the floor, then he looked up and nodded.

"I suppose you're right," McAfferty said. He picked up the three bills and carefully folded them in half. "I probably can help you. I think this town could use some new blood. A more aggressive attitude might be just what we need. So how are you going to find out what's happening down at the Johnson's farm?"

"Well, I'm not sure yet."

McAfferty glanced at his watch. "You figure out what's going on there, and I'll do my best to make sure this town gets a new sheriff. Understood?"

"Yes, sir," the deputy nodded his head excitedly.

"Good." McAfferty took the money, held it up, then pulled open his top desk drawer and placed the bills inside. "I'll hold onto the money for you."

The deputy stared at him with his mouth open, but he didn't say anything.

"We're done for now, deputy." McAfferty picked up a file from his desk and opened it. "Come back when you have something more for me."

He didn't look up as the deputy left the room.

.21.

Ralwil Turth

Ralwil Turth never realized it before, but he loved to sing. In his own body, singing was not a possibility. In his species, speech was an inefficient method of communication. It was much easier to communicate through gestures, or directly, mind to mind. Back home, he had the ability to speak in a way, but this was mostly in coarse squeaks and grunts, used to show enthusiasm or add emphasis to a conversation. But when he had taken on the body of the creatures here, these humans, he had to model their vocal cords too. Humans were very vocal creatures. If he wanted to fit in, he needed to be able to vocalize like they did. After synch-linking with Grady, he had learned the basics of their speech, but he always felt unsure of himself speaking in their tongue. He used speech when he had to, but he avoided it whenever he could. But that was before he learned how to sing. Now he wanted to vocalize all the time.

Part of it was the vibrations. When he sang, he felt the vibrations start down in his stomach when he took his first deep breath. Then they built up through his chest. He could feel the power growing. Then, when he released his breath slowly over the vocal cords, creating the sound, his head hummed with the vibrations. It made his whole body feel tingly. More than that, he liked the sound of his voice, and how he could control the sounds that came out. He liked to sing. He wondered why these humans did not do it more often.

That's what he had liked about church. Going in, he felt excited to be crowding in with all those humans. He had never seen this many people in one place at the same time, and he wondered what had brought them all together. So many different types of people. They came in all sizes—fat, thin, short, tall, some with long bushy hair, others with no hair at all.

He had gotten used to the appearance of these creatures. When he had first come here, all humans looked alike. Now he could easily tell them apart. It was the same with their voices. When they talked, the sound came out flat. But in the church, their voices all came together in a rich, powerful blend. The first time he heard it, he tingled from the vibrations. They made him want to sing along.

He still did not understand all the rules these humans lived by. That time at the church when everyone else was singing, Ralwil felt the energy build and he joined in. Then Grady dug his elbow into Ralwil's side and told him to do it softer. This made no sense. Singing loud was not hard at all.

Later, after they had moved out of the big room with the colored windows and gone into the smaller room where everyone just stood around, he felt the urge to sing again. The Ma was talking with two of the other females, but as soon as he started singing, she rushed over and guided him out of the building. All the people stared at him as he left the room. He wondered if he would ever completely understand these humans.

That seemed unlikely. If things worked out as he planned, he would not be here much longer. At night, after finishing dinner with the family grouping, he went back to the barn to work on his pod's power source. He had collected buckets of corn from the field, but this was just the first step. It was a piece of corn that had set off the detection device, but he was sure that it wasn't the corn itself but something inside the corn that made it work. He'd never seen corn in any other part of the universe.

Ralwil picked up a long length of tube and moved it around in his hands so he could see it from all sides. This could be useful in distilling the essence of the corn. If the corn worked well on its own, it would surely work even better if he was able to extract what was inside and concentrate it. He put down the tube and picked up an old copper kettle he'd found in a corner of the barn. He could easily break down the chemical composition of the corn by changing the settings on his replicator. But it would take power to do that. Power he didn't have.

Maybe he couldn't do this the easy way, but there was usually more than one way to solve a problem. Ralwil looked at the parts and pieces he'd collected in front of him. Junk, Grady had called it. He picked up a bottle and connected it with a coiled length of copper tube. If his projections were right, he had most of what he needed to make a machine that would convert the raw corn into a concentrated composite.

This could work, he thought. In fact, he knew it would work. It would take time and effort, but this was the answer. All he had to do was build the machine, process the corn to form the composite, and activate the core, and he could fix his pod and be on his way home. Ralwil felt a sense of joy well up in his stomach and spread through his body.

He took a deep breath and began to sing.

.23.

Deputy Schtinkle

Deputy Schtinkle hurried home right after he finished work, grabbed some things he needed for the stakeout, and put on his Ninja suit. It wasn't really a ninja suit, it was a pair of tight black jeans and a tight black shirt. But when he wore them together, they made him feel like a ninja. To complete the look, he pulled a black stocking cap over his head to cover his hair.

As he stared at himself in the mirror, he thought this might be a little much. He did look a little odd. When he wasn't wearing his uniform, he usually dressed in khakis and a comfortable button down shirt. This outfit was tight, different from the way he usually dressed, different from how anyone in town dressed. But once it got dark out in the Johnson's field, he would be as good as invisible. Just like a real ninja.

He looked out the window to make sure no one was around. Then he quietly slipped out the back door and made his way up front toward his car. Just as he rounded the side of the house, a car door slammed. Deputy Schtinkle froze. He thought about running back inside, but he was too late. Mrs. Rolland, his landlady, rounded the corner carrying a bag of groceries. Seeing him, she gasped. The bag slipped out of her hand and crashed to the ground. She quickly covered her mouth to hide a laugh.

Deputy Schtinkle hurried past her and out to his squad car without saying a word. He *knew* that was going to happen. He knew that if he wore the tight black outfit, someone was sure to see him. He *knew* that. Now Mrs. Rolland would tell the neighbors, and they would tell all their friends, and pretty soon everyone in town would be talking about how the young deputy dressed up in tight black clothes in his free time. How could he get respect if people were talking about him behind his back?

Still, he had a plan, and a job to do. He drove out of town, down Schmidt Road, all the way to the cornfields surrounding the Johnson farm. He might look strange, but the suit was just what he needed. It was already getting dark. No one would be able to see him now.

He pulled off the road and drove straight into the corn. The stalks crunched under his wheels. He drove a few yards further to make sure he was hidden from the road. Last time, he'd made the mistake of parking too far away from his target. Then, on the way back, he'd gotten lost in the cornfields and spent hours searching for the car. He wasn't going to let that happen again. He'd planned everything out this time. From where he sat, he could see the top of the barn in the distance. It would be a straight walk through the cornfield, and he wouldn't have to cut through thorny brambles or cross the creek. This time, his plan was foolproof.

He turned off the engine and checked his watch. He still had about half an hour until it was dark. He sat back and ate the sandwich he had brought along. This could be a long night. He would need his energy.

He waited until the sun was down and the sky had turned an inky black before getting out of the car. He quickly checked his supplies: his binoculars, a compass—to make absolutely sure he didn't get lost again—a canteen of water, and a camera. He was all set. Softly, he pushed the car door closed and slunk down to make sure he could not be seen above the top of the corn. Then he started toward the barn.

He had been moving for a while when he began to itch. At first he thought it was the corn. The thick green leaves and dangling tassels rubbed against him as he moved. He scratched at his back and tried to stoop down lower where the husks would not rub up against him. After a minute, though, his legs began to ache, and it did not really help. Now both his legs and his shoulders itched. Something buzzed by his ear, and he slapped at his neck. *Darn! Mosquitoes!* And because the fabric on his shirt was thin, they were biting right through. He gritted his teeth and kept on moving. He should have brought along bug spray.

He went a little farther, slapping at the bugs as he went, when he realized another thing he had forgotten, again. A flashlight, standard equipment on every cop's belt. It was so dark out here that, even though he knew where he was going, it was still hard to find his way. The moon was just a sliver in the sky, and all he could make out in front of him were shadowy images. He knew they were only cornstalks, but in the dark his imagination ran wild. They seemed to be moving. Maybe someone was in the cornfield with him, watching. No, he told himself. That could not be. *Every-*

thing is fine—there's nothing to worry about. But it was so dark now he could not make out the outline of the barn. His heart racing, he walked faster.

He was going in the right direction—he had aimed right for it and had not changed course—so he knew he was not lost. Or at least he hoped he was not. He heard a rustling sound in the corn. It sounded close. It might be the wind, or some small animal moving through, but what if it was something more sinister? He started to jog. But jogging elevated his heart rate, upped his blood pressure, and made him more anxious. Then, without realizing how it happened, he was running full speed.

He crashed through the cornstalks, flailing his arms and gasping for breath. He'd never felt so scared. He was running for his life. From what, he was not sure. He stumbled once, catching himself with his hand before he fell to the ground. Then he was up again. The binoculars bounced back and forth against his chest and he could hardly breathe. He wasn't used to running, and he didn't think he could go on much longer. He fought the urge to look back and see if the thing was gaining on him. Then, suddenly, he was out of the corn.

The barn was in front of him, right past a great big tree, and the house was off to the side. Nothing moved in the quiet corn. A soft breeze rustled the leaves on the tree and whispered through the cornstalks. He took a deep breath. There was nothing back there. It had all been his imagination. He was glad that no one was around to see him. It was bad enough that Mrs. Rolland had seen him in his black outfit. If word leaked out that he had panicked while walking in a corn field, he would never hear the end of it.

Stay calm, he told himself. *Relax.* He put his hands on his knees, bent over, and tried to catch his breath. He was more than winded; he felt exhausted. His heart boomed and his knees felt wobbly. He needed to sit down for a minute and recover. He stumbled forward to the base of the tree and leaned against its trunk. He had to get himself together. Propped up against the tree trunk, he gulped in the air. After a few minutes, he felt himself calm down. His breath returned to normal. This wasn't so bad, he thought. Here he was, right on the Johnson farm, in the heart of enemy territory, right where he wanted to be. *What now?* He should explore the area, maybe get into the barn and see what was going on there.

He was just about to get up when a light went on near the house and he heard the sound of a screen door slamming closed. *Someone was coming.* Deputy Schtinkle flattened himself against the tree and felt its rough bark dig into his back. He held his breath and tried to keep still. He hoped his black suit was doing its trick and that he looked invisible. Soon he heard footsteps and a soft humming. He hoped that whoever it was wasn't coming in his direction. He held his breath and tried to stay as still as a statue. After a few moments his curiosity got the best of him and he turned and looked to see who it was. It was the big farmhand. He carried a flashlight and looked straight ahead as he strolled toward the barn.

Deputy Schtinkle watched as the man unlocked the barn door and stepped inside. A second later, a light went on. This was exciting. Now all he had to do was creep up and look inside. With a little luck, he could catch the farmhand in the act—whatever that act was.

Deputy Schtinkle stood up and cautiously moved toward the barn. He stared into the shadows, trying to see if anyone was there. He still wasn't sure what was going on, but he felt puzzled. He had expected to see guards posted nearby, maybe criminal types, or even Columbian drug runners. But it didn't look as if anyone else was nearby. In a way, that was disappointing.

As he got closer to the barn, he heard a dog barking up at the house. *Drat!* He felt his muscles tense. He had never liked dogs, and the thought of a dog chasing after him made his stomach queasy. He should have expected they would have a dog. All the farmers kept dogs. Next time he would have to bring along some dog biscuits or other treats, or maybe some pepper spray in case the dog attacked him. But it was too late for that now. All he could do now was hope they kept the dog inside.

The dog kept on barking. Deputy Schtinkle's stomach turned again. *What was it barking at? Him?* That could not be good. If it kept on barking, sooner or later someone inside would have to let it out. He looked around for a place to hide.

The barn was close by, and that was where he wanted to be anyway. Maybe he could sneak inside without the big farmhand seeing him. He took another step forward, but just as he did, a loud thundering sound came from inside the barn. Deputy Schtinkle jumped back. It sounded like a fog horn, only it kept on going. It had to be an alarm they had put up. Somehow he had set it off. He spun around. Now they would surely release the dog. There had to be some place close where he could hide. Then he remembered the tree at the edge of the cornfield. Its branches were low enough to climb. He didn't like the idea of being stuck up in the tree with the dog barking below, but he couldn't think of a better idea. He scurried back toward the tree.

He only went a few steps before he stopped. The dog was still barking, and the alarm was still blaring, only in a different pitch now. But something else was wrong. He felt the hair on the back of his neck stand on end. *What was it?*

Deputy Schtinkle looked around and didn't notice anything different. He sniffed the air. Nothing seemed out of place there either. He couldn't place what it was, but he couldn't help feeling that something was different. He started moving again, slowly now, trying to make his way over to the tree. His eyes had adjusted to the dark and he could see a little, but not much.

Once he was within yards of the tree, he started to relax. The dog was still inside.

No one was responding to the alarm. Maybe this was going to work out okay after all. Then he saw a flash of white just a few feet in front of him—he realized at once that the white was the stripe on a skunk's back. He froze in his tracks, but it was too late. The skunk was in position, its rear end aimed at him like a pistol. Deputy Schtinkle covered his face as the skunk let go. The spray hit him full on. He fell to the ground, gasping for breath.

He rolled on the ground, gagging and choking for what seemed like forever. Finally, he was able to breathe again. He sat up and rubbed the tears out of his eyes. It seemed quieter now. The dog had stopped barking. The alarm was still going, but now it sounded almost musical. Slowly, he stood up, walked past the tree, and headed back into the cornfield.

Deputy Schtinkle hung his head and started back to look for his car. With his luck he would never find it.

.24.

Ralwil Turth

Ralwil checked the seal on the side of a bubbling jug to make sure it was tight and free of leaks. He'd been working on the contraption for weeks. Now it was fully operational.

"This is really great, Will. What does it do?" Grady asked. He walked around the barn, looking at Rawil's finished creation.

"Concentrates corn," Will said. "Makes it work better."

"Wow! This is amazing. It looks like something out of a cartoon, almost like a machine a mad scientist would make."

Ralwil had spent all his spare time working on the machine. He saw what he needed clearly in his mind before he started assembling it. He linked together some tubes and bottles, brass couplings, and parts of an old transmission. Some of the things he had found at the hardware store. Other materials he scavenged from around the home. The device used a combination of biological, chemical, and mechanical processes, and he had tubes snaking across the floor, hooked up to cans and bottles he had placed on shelves at different levels. He had built valves and regulators, and had fashioned the device to take advantage of the natural flow of gravity. At one end of the contraption, he mixed the raw corn with the other components in a big metal bucket. Then he used the Q-Provenator from his omnibelt to provide the energy needed to start the process. Slowly the mixture worked its way through the contraption, dripping out the other end and solidifying as a highly concentrated composite. The device looked odd, and it was not as efficient as he would have liked, but it worked well enough.

Ralwil went through the barn, checking the stages of the process. It worked slowly, but the composite was starting to build, drip by drip. At this rate, in another week or two he would have enough material to repair the power source. And then he would take off, leaving this planet behind, and finally head home.

Grady followed Ralwil around, checking the seals and connections too. Ralwil liked having him around. The boy liked to help, and Ralwil liked to hear him talk. He learned so much of what this world was like by listening to him.

"How did you learn to make all this stuff, Will? Was your Dad handy, or did you have a job doing stuff like this?"

Ralwil shook his head. He didn't know how he knew what he knew. Some of it was training and experience, other things he had always known. They were shared memories from his swarm, collective experiences that were ingrained in him.

"My dad taught me a lot too. That's why I'm pretty handy," Grady said. "He could fix just about anything."

Ralwil finished checking the machine. It was set up and working just as he had expected. When he had first landed on this planet, he'd had no idea how he was going to survive, or how he could ever fix his pod and get back home. Now he had not only survived, he had come to know these native creatures and appreciate them. He had helped them. He had turned what could have been a disaster into one of the best experiences of his life.

Ralwil turned around. The expression on Grady's face had changed. His big smile was gone and his eyes looked different. Ralwil tilted his head. Something was wrong. The boy was happy before, and now he wasn't. Ralwil didn't know why, but he sensed that the boy was in pain of some kind. It was strange. Then he realized that he felt bad too, and that he felt bad because Grady felt bad. This was a new feeling for him.

"Sorry." Grady wiped his eyes. "I was just thinking about my dad. Sometimes I really miss him."

Ralwil stood still. He wished he could do something to take away this young boy's pain. He didn't know what to do. Then, without thinking or even knowing why he did it, Ralwil walked forward and put his hand on the boy's shoulder.

Grady reached up and gripped Ralwil's hand.

"Thanks, Will," he said. "I'm glad you're here."

Ralwil squeezed back. He was glad he was there, too. He looked forward to going back home, but he was glad he was here now. He would miss this boy when he did have to go.

.25.

McAfferty

Every morning, before opening the bank, McAfferty stopped at the Busy Bee for a cup of coffee. It was not that the coffee there was so good, though it wasn't bad. The Busy Bee was the meeting place for all the local businessmen, and McAfferty went there to get a line on the local gossip. It was almost a ritual. Every morning he would walk in the door at eight thirty-five and take a seat at the long front counter. The waitress would pour his coffee without his having to ask.

Then he would nod his head at the others gathered there and sit back to listen. By listening closely to the gossip, he got a feel for the pulse of the community, for what was really going on. It was here that he first found out that the Allen brothers were looking to expand, and it was here that he had learned about George Struther's cash flow problem, long before it showed up on his balance sheet.

McAfferty sat down at the end of the counter, next to Morretti, the grocer, who was talking loudly with Jim Baker, the manager of the auto parts store. Patti, the mousy young waitress, came by. She flipped his cup and filled it without even looking at him.

He nodded, took a small sip, and turned toward the conversation.

"It stunk so bad, it got into my nostrils and I couldn't sleep," Morretti said. "After he left, I scrubbed down the sidewalk with bleach, but I could still smell it. When I got home, Rose made me take a shower right away. I think I'm going to have to burn my clothes."

"It was that bad?"

"It was worse than that. I couldn't even breathe. He came by right after closing time and banged on the window. Once I got a whiff of it, I wouldn't let him inside. I made him walk down the block. I went to the shelf and pulled out all the tomato juice we had and left it out by the door for him. I wouldn't even take his money. I'll get it later, I told him. You wouldn't believe how bad it smelled."

"Does that work?" Baker asked.

"What?"

"The tomato juice. Does that really take away the smell?"

"How should I know?" Morretti replied. "I never got sprayed by a skunk."

Then someone down the counter said that vinegar worked better, and another person said the only way to get rid of the smell was with hydrogen peroxide, but by then McAfferty had lost interest in the conversation. He wondered who the poor sap was, but it did not concern him. He took another small sip of his coffee—it was hot enough to burn his tongue—and thought about going into work early. He was here for information, and this type of news didn't help him at all. He had hoped they might still be talking about the Johnsons, the biggest topic lately. But since they'd last come into town, there hadn't been any new news.

Others had lost interest, McAfferty thought, but not him. He wanted to know where that money had come from. Money like that didn't just grow on trees. There was no way to keep a secret in a small town like this. If someone was up to something, it wouldn't be long before everyone else knew about it. So how were the Johnsons keeping their secret?

"Well, what I want to know is what was he doing sneaking around by that skunk anyway?" This was Baker again. He was big and brawny, but he spoke in a high squeaky voice. "My sister-in-law, Mimi Rolland—he boards with her—saw him last night dressed up in some kind of black outfit. She said she couldn't stop laughing. He looked like Batman, only real skinny and all."

"That's right!" Morretti said excitedly. "That's what he was dressed like when he came by the store. He was in some kind of black outfit. I don't think he even had any pockets!"

McAfferty tuned out the conversation. He wondered what the deputy was doing. He hadn't heard from him since his visit to the office last week. He knew he couldn't count on him, but there was no way McAfferty could investigate the Johnsons himself, so he had no choice but to rely on the deputy. At least he had the desire, and sometimes that was enough. With a little luck, he would stumble across something at the Johnson farm and it would all come together. The more he thought about it, the more he liked the idea of the deputy solving the mystery. He had promised him he would support him for sheriff. He clearly wasn't qualified, but it would be nice to have someone in charge who he could control, someone who knew who the real boss was.

He took another small sip. The coffee had hardly cooled down at all. He blew on the cup before setting it back down.

"Why would someone go around dressed like that? That's what I want to know."

Baker's voice sounded like he had been inhaling helium, almost like a cartoon character.

"I don't know. I wouldn't be caught dead wearing something like that."

"Me neither. I mean, not out in public." The conversation stopped. McAfferty looked over. Everyone was looking at Baker. Baker quickly cleared his throat. "I mean, I wouldn't be caught dead wearing that either."

McAfferty smiled. He took another sip of his coffee. "Who are you talking about?" he asked.

"It's that new deputy, Deputy Schtinkle." Morretti replied. Then he launched in on the whole story again, how the deputy had banged on his windows after closing time, and how he had reacted, and so on. But McAfferty stopped listening. Hearing the deputy's name, he fumbled with his coffee cup and hot coffee spilled onto his leg. He grabbed a fistful of napkins and mopped at the spill. *God, that was hot!*

It was all Helen Johnson's fault. If she hadn't been so dif-ficult, he wouldn't have had to rely on the deputy, who obviously couldn't do anything right. He needed to take care of this problem, and he couldn't rely on anyone else. If he wanted this done right, he would have to do it himself.

.26.

Ralwil Turth

Sparks rose up in the air like fireflies, floating higher and higher until they seemed to blend in with the stars. Ralwil watched the sparks rise and imagined that he was one of them, floating up high into space and drifting on. It was a still, warm night and he sat with the family group in front of a roaring fire.

It was such a beautiful night that after dinner the Ma had suggested that they have a bonfire in the fire pit near the road at the front of the house. Grady and Luanne gathered up wood and the Ma started the blaze. Then they all sat in a circle around the fire, watching the flames dance, everyone quiet. The logs crackled and popped, but otherwise the night was calm.

Ralwil leaned in closer so he could feel the heat on his face. This was nice. He felt more at peace now than at any time since he had landed on this strange and wonderful planet.

Earlier in the day, he had checked the progress of the composite machine, and the tubs were nearly full. Another day, maybe two, and he would have enough material to fix the power supply. Just a few more days and he could go home.

Ralwil reached his hands toward the fire and closed his eyes. The heat reminded him of the time he had toured the volcanic regions of Wyn Turxx back home, and how the intense heat had warmed him through to his core. The smell of burning wood here was much more pleasant than the sulfur smell back then, but the heat triggered thoughts of home. Ralwil wondered what it would feel like to breathe his own air again, to feel the warmth of his own sun and the deep connection with his swarm mates. Would it still be the same after all the time he been away, after all he had seen? All at once he had a fierce longing to be back, to touch the ground of his home planet.

"Summer is almost gone," the Ma said, breaking the quiet. "School will be starting in just over a week."

"It's too soon," Grady groaned. "I don't want to go back to

school yet. It's been a good summer. There's never been a summer like this before."

"I want school to start," Luanne said. "I miss my friends."

"We have to get everything ready for school," the Ma said. "And it's almost harvest time too."

Ralwil grunted. He didn't mean to grunt. He meant to say how much he had enjoyed the summer and how much he appreciated the family and his time with them. He wanted to tell them he would be leaving soon, and how he would always remember them. He wanted to let them know exactly how he felt. He tried again, but he was filled with new emotions and couldn't make himself speak. Another grunt came out.

The Ma, Grady, and Luanne all looked at him. Ralwil knew he had to say something to the family group, but he didn't want to just make strange noises again. He kept his mouth shut.

"Who is ready for s'mores?" the Ma broke in.

"I am," Luanne cried.

"Me too," said Grady.

Ralwil wasn't sure what a *smorz* was, but he wanted one too. Grady had already gathered long sticks that had fallen from the big tree, and peeled the bark off one end. He gave one of the sticks to each of them. The Ma pulled out a plastic bag filled with small white cylinders. She passed one of the cylinders over to each of them.

"Can I have another?" Luanne asked.

"Yes, but let's start with one at a time."

Ralwil watched as they each stuck a white cylinder onto the end of a stick, then moved the stick over the fire. Ralwil turned the cylinder over in his hand. It felt hard and chalky on the outside, but when he squeezed it, it was soft and squishy. He knew this was some sort of foodstuff, but it looked nothing like any of the foods they grew here on the farm. He poked the cylinder onto his stick and it slid right on. The others all had their sticks extended over the fire. It looked dangerous, but the Ma was doing it too, so it had to be safe. He reached the stick out so the cylinder was just over the top of the flame and waited to see what happened next. The fire here seemed different from the fire he'd experienced in other galaxies, maybe because of the fuel they used. The bright orange and red colors were calming and made him feel peaceful. The way the flames moved, they almost seemed alive.

"Will! Your marshmallow is burning! Quick, blow it out." Grady's voice cut through his thoughts.

He pulled his stick back and stared with amazement at the blob on the end of his stick. It burned like a torch.

Luanne laughed. "Come on, Will. Blow it out or you'll ruin it."

Ralwil didn't want to ruin the smorz, so he took a deep breath and blew at the flame as hard as he could. The fire went out, leaving a blackened, melting glob. It looked strange and unappealing. He wondered what he was supposed to do with it now.

"It's a little charred, but it should still be fine." The Ma passed him two thin brown squares and a smaller dark rectangle.

"Haven't you had these before, Will? They're great." Grady reached over to help. "Here, you just slide this altogether so everything is in the middle." Grady used one of the squares to pry the glob off the stick and sandwiched it together with the other.

Ralwil looked at it closely, then took a big bite of the strange concoction. The outside crunched. Then he bit into the hot, gooey center. It was sticky and creamy and sharply sweet. This was like nothing he had tasted before. He took another bite and closed his eyes. The smorz oozed out and dripped over his fingers, sticking against his skin. This was another thing he would miss, these new experiences that still happened nearly every day. He would relay this experience to his swarm mates, but it wouldn't come across nearly as powerfully as he felt it now. He would miss this place.

"I'll have another, please," Luanne said.

"You want another, Grady? Are you ready yet, Will?" the Ma asked.

Ralwil stared at the fire and watched the sparks dance. Yes, he would miss this place. He would miss the taste of potatoes, the smell of newly mowed grass, and the sweet and crunchy taste of smorz. But most of all he would miss this family grouping. He admired the Ma for her strength and courage, and he felt so comfortable with Grady and Luanne that they seemed almost like swarm mates. He would miss Ruthie too, and the smooth feel of her soft, warm fur against his hand. He was not sure what this was, but he felt connected to this family grouping in a way he had never felt before.

Ralwil opened his mouth to talk. He had to tell the family how he felt. He had to tell them good-bye. He opened his mouth wide, but no sound came out. Summer was over. The kids were going back to school, and he was leaving forever, going home.

Ralwil tried to think of what to say and how to say it.

"Are you ready yet, Will?" Without waiting for a reply, the

Ma passed over another cylinder of smorz.

But he wasn't leaving yet. Ralwil picked up the raw smorz. When the time came, he would say good-bye. This was not the time. He stuck the smorz on the end of his stick and moved it over the fire.

.27.

Grady

Grady was in the front yard reading when the letter came. Most days Mr. Hurly, the mailman, came by the farm around two in the afternoon. He always drove up the driveway and brought the mail straight up to the porch. If Ma was around, and she had time, she would offer him a cup of water or lemonade, and they'd stand around and talk for a little while. But this time Mr. Hurly said he was in a rush. He needed Ma to sign for a letter. They'd never had a letter that had to be signed for before, and Grady wondered what it was. He knew it had to be something important.

Grady ran out to the south field where Ma and Will were working. She was up on the tractor and didn't hear him at first, but once he got her attention she came right down and he told her about the letter. She didn't say anything, but Grady could tell by the look on her face that this wasn't good news. When they got back to the house, she signed, then opened the letter up right on the porch. Her eyes went wide. She sat down on the rocking chair.

Grady stood there watching her, waiting for her to say something, but she didn't speak for the longest time. He fidgeted around with his hands in his pockets. He wanted to say something to make her feel better, but he didn't know what to say. After a while, she finally looked up at him.

In a soft voice she said, "Run along now, Grady. Go see what your sister is doing."

"Okay, Ma," he said.

Grady went out back and kicked the dust around. It didn't seem fair. Just when it looked like all their problems were over, another one showed up. He hadn't seen the letter, but the envelope showed it was from the bank. Grady didn't know what the problem was, but he knew it had something to do with money again. He looked around for Luanne for a minute, but he didn't look hard. He didn't really care if he found her or not.

He headed over to the money tree. It hadn't grown any more

since its first spurt, but it stood nearly as tall as the oak tree out front. It was quiet except for a soft breeze that rustled through the leaves. It sounded like whispering. Grady looked up into the tree. The leaves were so thick, he couldn't see the sky. The lower branches, where they'd picked the leaves off before going to town, had grown new leaves. There was more money in that tree than he could imagine. He couldn't understand how they could have a problem, now that they had the money tree.

After a while, Grady went back inside. Ma was back out in the field, but she had left the letter on the counter. This wasn't his letter, but he knew it meant trouble for the family and he had to know what it said. He looked around, feeling guilty, then picked it up. The letter wasn't written with normal words, but used long words Grady had never even heard before. Still, after reading it through twice, he had a good idea of what the letter meant. The letter explained that if someone fell behind on their payments, the bank could demand that they pay off the entire balance of the loan at once. The bank was telling Ma that she had to pay the entire mortgage now, instead of making payments every month. Grady looked at the amount and knew that they would need ten money trees to come up with that kind of money all at one time.

Grady stayed out of Ma's way for the rest of the day. He felt bad that he'd read the letter, and he was sure she would be in a dark mood. But by dinnertime it seemed like she was back to normal. As they sat around the table, Luanne talked about a book she'd been reading and how funny it was. She went into a long explanation of the plot and what the characters said, using different voices for each one. When she talked about the King, her voice got really deep and it sounded funny. Ma asked questions about the book and laughed at the funny parts. Grady laughed too, and so did Will, but Grady wasn't sure Will knew what they were laughing about.

Grady started thinking that maybe things were going to be all right after all. When they'd finished dinner and were clearing off the dishes, Ma commented on how nice a night it was, and how it would be a waste to just spend it sitting around at home. There was a band concert in town. She thought it would be fun to go. So they all piled into the car and headed into town.

The concert was in the big veteran's park near the center of town. By the time they got there, the sun was nearly down, but the street lamps hadn't come on yet, and the light was golden. They parked the car and walked past the memorial garden with all its brightly colored flowers, into the park. The night was hot and muggy, and it really felt like summer. They followed the path past the playground and the softball field. The air smelled like flowers and freshly mowed grass.

At the center of the park, a big wooden stage was set up on the grass where the big fountain used to be. The band, the Community Brass Band, was up on the stage, sitting on plastic chairs arranged in a semicircle. They hadn't started playing yet, but they all had their instruments out and were tuning up. Grady liked how the instruments glowed in the golden light, and he liked listening to the honks and wheezes as the band tuned up. A big crowd had gathered to hear them. It seemed like half the town was there. Some people had set up lawn chairs, others had spread out big blankets.

As they moved into the crowd looking for a place to sit, the family passed by lots of people they knew. Some greeted them by name, others nodded and said hello. A few of them glanced strangely at Will, but Grady thought that by now people had heard enough about him that they weren't surprised to see him.

Ma found an open space next to the Sanders family, and they spread out their blankets. Mrs. Sanders and Ma were friends, and the Sanders had a daughter about Luanne's age. They all started chattering right away. Grady sat on the other blanket with Will.

Will looked around, his eyes wide. Grady wondered what he'd think of the music, but Ma had told him before they came that he couldn't sing—people thought he was strange enough as it was.

After a few minutes the conductor, Mr. Hanratty, the high school music teacher, stepped up to the microphone and thanked everyone for coming. He talked for another minute or two. Then he turned around and raised his baton and everyone got quiet as the music began to play. Grady had expected to hear a marching song like the ones the high school band played in parades. This music was something different. The sound was smooth and rich and powerful. The drums kept a beat like a slow-moving freight train. The horns sounded like a choir.

Ma closed her eyes and swayed back and forth to the music with a smile on her face. Seeing her happy like this, Grady thought about things she'd said before. It was the simple things in life that mattered, she'd said, and on a night like this you didn't need money to make you happy. Life felt perfect just like it was.

The band had just started their second song when Grady heard someone come up behind him. He turned around and saw Eddie Hobbes, a friend he hadn't seen since school let out.

"Grady, come on," Eddie said. "We're playing Red Rover

back by the playground, and we need another person."

Grady looked over at Ma, and she nodded her head. He looked at Will to see if he wanted to join them, but he was swaying to the music, a big smile on his face.

Grady jumped up and ran with Eddie, dodging between the blankets to the open field. It was darker now and lightning bugs were out, blinking in the thick summer air. It felt good to run, and Grady looked at the people as he ran past them. It seemed like everybody was smiling. Well, maybe not everyone. At the back, as Grady joined up with all the other kids and started playing, a skinny deputy sheriff stared at them. His arms were crossed and there was a scowl on his face. But they weren't doing anything wrong, and they were having too much fun just being out and enjoying summer to worry. They kept on playing Red Rover, and after a while the deputy walked away. Grady wished that night would never end.

.28.

Deputy Schtinkle

Deputy Stinky. He knew that was what they were calling him behind his back. He had heard the whispers in the diner, and watched as people covered their mouths to hide their smiles as he walked past. Even the sheriff was doing it. The other day he had called him Deputy Stinky in front of the whole department. He corrected himself right away, but he was smiling when he did it, and his apology did not seem sincere. Deputy Schtinkle wondered if he would ever live this down. It was bad enough to be sprayed by the skunk, but to have everyone in the whole town know about it, that was the worst.

Deputy Schtinkle walked past the play area and kept to the

outskirts of the crowd.

A bunch of kids were playing some kind of game in the field in back of the playground. They ran around shouting and laughing, and he was sure they were up to trouble of some kind. He gave them a hard look and waited for them to take the hint and move along. When they ignored him and kept on playing, he thought about rounding them up and giving them a warning. But he wasn't sure what he would warn them about. And besides, if any of them ran back and told their parents, it could be misinterpreted and he would look like a fool again. No, he couldn't risk that. He walked away, back through the crowd, looking for signs of trouble.

This was a waste of time anyway. Crowd control, the Sheriff had called it, but all he was doing was walking around feeling stupid. There were no problems here now, and there would be none later. It made no sense that he had to be *here* instead of out looking for real criminals. He knew he was on to something at the Johnson farm. He just needed a break to find out what it was. If he hadn't bumped into that skunk, he would have solved the case that night. It was all a matter of luck, and lately, his luck had all been bad. He walked around the blankets and lawn chairs, looking for anything out of the ordinary.

About halfway up to the stage he caught sight of the Johnsons' farm hand. Deputy Schtinkle slowed down and tried to look inconspicuous. The Johnson woman was right next to him, and there were two young girls chatting away next to her. He had never seen the whole family, but when he'd been out there last week, he hadn't seen any others. Was it possible that the whole gang was here tonight?

He tried to control his excitement. This could be his opportunity to solve the mystery once and for all. The Sheriff had warned him about following up on the Johnson case. After the skunk incident, he warned him again not to pursue it any further. And the banker, McAfferty, wasn't even taking his calls anymore. So if he moved forward with this investigation, he was on his own. If he did this and got caught, that would be the end of his law enforcement career in this town. And forever after he would be known as Stinky. So the risks were big. But no one ever got ahead by playing it safe. He saw it on the detective shows every week. All the great detectives broke the rules and took the risks to make the big bust. If he was going to be a great detective, he needed to take some risks too.

He felt his adrenaline surge as he cut through the crowd and headed out of the park.

If the whole Johnson gang was here, he would have to act fast. He had to make his move before they left and went back to the farm. Once out of the crowd, he ran down the path to the street where he had parked his squad car.

He nearly gagged when he opened the door and the smell hit him again. He had cleaned the car with Lysol, twice, let it air out, and used every air freshener he could buy, but it still reeked of skunk. The Sheriff had an old squad car that they didn't use because it needed new tires and a paint job. Deputy Schtinkle had pleaded with him to let him use that car for a while, but the Sheriff said no. The Sheriff thought the whole thing was funny. Now he'd see who had the last laugh. Deputy Schtinkle rolled down the windows and started the engine. He pulled a U-turn and raced toward the Johnson farm.

As he got closer, he thought about where he could park. He had to be careful to find a place where they wouldn't see his car when they came back. He drove past their driveway and pulled off the road, well into the corn. Then he cut his lights, got out, and backtracked to the driveway. He was still in his uniform. If anyone saw him, he would have some real explaining to do. But no one would see him—they were all at the concert. At least he hoped they were. The gravel crunched under his feet and the sound made him nervous. He looked up ahead. The front porch light was on, but the house was dark. So far, so good. He hurried forward as quietly as he could.

As he passed the house, a dog barked inside. Deputy Schtinkle froze. *He'd forgotten about the dog!* His breath caught in his chest and he felt light-headed. For a second he was afraid he would faint. The dog kept barking, but no lights went on, and no doors opened. After a minute, Deputy Schtinkle regained his courage and continued past the house and on toward the big barn. He hadn't thought to bring his flashlight along.

Again! But the moon was nearly full, and he could see clearly without it. He looked into the shadows by the barn, searching for any sign of guards. It looked all clear. He didn't know what the Johnson gang was up to, but they had to be feeling cocky to leave their barn unguarded.

At the barn door, he examined the latch. It was locked with a cheap padlock. Some time back, he had sent away for a mail order course on lock picking. The ad claimed that with a little practice he could easily learn to dismantle any lock. But he'd never had time to read the book. He had, however, remembered to bring a screwdriver from the car. He forced the screwdriver through the lock and twisted with all his strength. The lock held, but he felt something give. The latch screws had loosened from the barn door. He pried at it again, and this time it gave way. He pulled the broken latch free and opened the door. As soon as the Johnsons saw that, they would know someone had broken in. But by then it would no longer matter. He would have the evidence. He'd be ready for the arrest.

Stepping inside the barn, he couldn't see a thing. Other than the crack of light from the door, it was pitch black. He imagined that someone was inside now, watching him. He felt a lump in his throat and swallowed. There had to be some kind of light here. He remembered seeing one shining when the big farmhand went in the week before, right before he had tripped the alarm. Deputy Schtinkle reached his hands out and fumbled to find the wall. After a step or two he felt rough wood against his fingers. He slid his hand down the wall, looking for a light switch. Suddenly something bit his hand.

"Ow!" he cried out, pulling his finger back to his mouth. It wasn't a bite, he realized, but a sliver of wood. He'd have to be more careful. He put his hand out again and moved it more carefully up and down the wall. It took a few minutes, but he found the switch. He turned it on and the barn was flooded with light. He blinked a few times as his eyes adjusted to the brightness, then looked around. At first he saw nothing unusual. A big old farm tractor was parked at the entrance and, against the wall close to the door, a large work bench overflowed with tools and junk. Next to that was a tall shelving unit packed with more stuff. The place was a mess. It needed organization, but it didn't look like the criminal lair he had expected.

Actually, Deputy Schtinkle wasn't sure what he expected to find. Well, money for one thing. And maybe drugs, or stolen merchandise, or guns, or even gold bars. Could be most anything. He once heard a story about a man who lived in a small apartment in some big city. The man kept to himself, and all the neighbors thought he was a nice guy, just real quiet. The man had a little dog that he walked through the neighborhood every day. Then one day the guy had an accident or something and was hospitalized so he wasn't able to walk his dog. His neighbors heard the dog whining, so they got the apartment manager to open up the apartment to get the dog out. The apartment was stacked from floor to ceiling with stolen shoes. Thousands of them. Deputy Schtinkle didn't think the Johnson barn would be filled with shoes, but it wouldn't surprise him if it were.

He walked around the tractor so he could see the rest of the barn. Big hay bales were stacked up like a staircase. The air smelled dusty, and it tickled his nose. He thought he was going to sneeze, but he didn't. He sniffed again and smelled something strange. It wasn't a bad smell, but it seemed out of place. He couldn't place it, but it reminded him of midways at the county fair. He walked past the tractor to the back of the barn. His mouth dropped open in surprise.

He had never seen anything like it. It looked like the kind of machine mad scientists made on Saturday morning cartoons. It took up most of the back portion of the barn. At one end a big covered vat sat on a shelf. Leading from that was a series of tubes, bubbling with a bluish liquid. These tubes snaked around in different directions, connecting with bottles and cans, looping around in strange configurations with little motors, fans, and valves connecting them. The contraption gave off a low humming noise—so low he hadn't even noticed it when he'd first come into the barn. This machine was the source of the smell. All at once he recognized what the smell reminded him of.

Cotton candy! The contraption smelled like cotton candy!

Deputy Schtinkle carefully walked around the machine. He'd seen stills on TV where people made moonshine whiskey, but they didn't look anything like this. He'd heard about labs that made drugs, but he'd never heard that they smelled like cotton candy. This had to be something like that, but what? Whatever it was, it sure as heck couldn't be legal. Whatever it was, it had to be part of the plot. It was evidence. But without knowing what it was, or what it did, what could he charge the Johnsons with?

Deputy Schtinkle pondered this for a minute and came up with a plan. Finding the contraption by itself was not enough. To make the charge stick, to find out all the details of the plot, he would have to catch them red-handed. He had seen enough cases in the movies and on TV to know how the system worked. He would wait until the culprits were inside, using the machine. Then he'd come in with his pistol drawn and confront them. Once they saw that they were caught, they would confess and give up all the evidence. The plan couldn't be any simpler.

But to make his plan work, he needed a good place to hide. He looked around the barn. On top of the hay bales, he could lie down and they probably wouldn't see him from the door. But as they moved around, he would be exposed. Besides, inside the barn he wouldn't know what he was up against until he saw them come in. It would be better to be outside where he could see how many there were when they came back. That way he could observe them safely. Then he would be ready to move when they entered the barn, and he wouldn't be caught off guard. And if he was going to be outside, the perfect hiding place would be behind that big tree.

Deputy Schtinkle hurried back around the tractor to the front of the barn and turned off the lights. He waited a few seconds for his eyes to get used to the dark. Then he glanced outside to make sure the coast was clear. It looked okay as far as he could tell, so he stepped out and closed the barn door behind him. He looked at the latch. The lock was unopened, but it hung to the side where he had forced it. If they saw that, they would know someone had been inside and that would ruin the surprise. He pushed the screws into the loose wood so it looked like it had before. He hoped it would not fall off when they went to unlock it. There was nothing much else he could do.

He took a deep breath and ran back over to the tree. His heart was pounding as he squatted down and prepared to wait. This was sweet. The sheriff and the others had laughed at him, but he would have the last laugh. After they saw how he'd solved the case, they would look at him differently. Then they would see him for the hero he truly was. After a few minutes of squatting, his thighs started to hurt, so he sat down and leaned back against the trunk of the tree. He didn't know how long he would have to wait, and it made no sense to tire himself out before he needed to. This could be a long night. It would pay to conserve his energy. When they showed up, he would hear the car and see the lights. Then he would get in position.

Deputy Schtinkle tried to relax. It was awfully quiet now. The dog up at the house had stopped its barking, and the only sounds were the serenade of crickets and cicadas. It was really quite soothing. After all the excitement, it felt good to rest. After a while, he was totally relaxed. He yawned. As time dragged by, it was hard to keep his focus. They were taking longer to get back then he had anticipated. He checked his watch. The concert should have been over by now. *What was keeping them?* He yawned again. He hadn't realized how tired he was. He hadn't gotten enough sleep the last few nights, and with all the excitement, he guessed it had worn down his system. It was hard to keep his eyes open. He couldn't fall asleep, but he needed to rest his eyes. He'd just close them for a minute. Then he'd feel more alert and be ready to go when they came back.

He'd hear the car. His adrenaline would kick in again and he'd be set for whatever happened. He yawned again and let his eyes close.

The next thing he knew, a bird was singing close to his ear, the sky was light, and the flame orange sun was peeking up over the corn field. Deputy Schtinkle shook his head. *Had he fallen asleep?* It didn't seem possible. He'd only closed his eyes for a second, but he must have, and now it was dawn. His mouth was dry and tasted like dog food. His body ached and his neck felt cramped. He looked toward the house. The Johnsons' car was sitting in the driveway. *Darn!* He had missed them again. *How was it possible?* All he needed to do was stay awake, and he couldn't even do that. He stood up, stretched, and kicked a clod of dirt as hard as he could. *So what now?* Not much. For all he knew, the crooks were on to him and he'd lost any chance at surprise. He'd messed it up again.

Deputy Schtinkle yawned again and rubbed the sleep from his eyes. Probably the best thing now was to go back to town and act as if nothing had happened. It hurt to admit defeat. He stretched again and his eyes happened on a low hanging branch of the tree in front of him. His vision was still blurry from sleep, but something didn't seem right. He rubbed his eyes and looked again. At once, his heart started pounding. He pinched himself to make sure he was awake.

The pinch hurt, so he knew he wasn't dreaming. Then his knees turned to jelly. He wobbled unsteadily and fell down on the ground.

As he looked up, the leaves in the tree fluttered in a fresh breeze—every one of them a twenty dollar bill.

.29.

McAfferty

Though all the regulars were there, seated in their usual places, the diner seemed quieter than normal. The noise was muted, as if
people had all stayed up too late the night before and were having a
hard time waking up this morning. Or maybe that was just the way
he felt. But the quiet suited him. It gave him time to think, and he
wasn't in the mood to talk with anybody.

He picked up his spoon and swirled the cream in his coffee
as he looked down the counter. Morretti the grocer was there. So
was Jim Baker from the auto parts store. A couple of old farmers
were huddled together at the end of the counter, complaining about
crop prices. The rest of the room was full too. At a table in the mid-

dle, Old Man Harris and the other old-timers were silently eating their oatmeal. The Ganders brothers from the pharmacy sat around the table sneering at each other in their matching white coats. In all the time he had known them, McAfferty still could not tell one brother from another. He glanced over toward the door. Al Freely, the car dealer, was there. When McAfferty first came in, he'd noticed Freely slide down in his seat and cover his face with a menu. Freely was constantly behind in his payments and always avoided him. On a normal day, McAfferty would have gone over and reminded him. This morning it didn't seem worth the bother, and he was in no mood for a confrontation.

He took another sip of coffee and let his mind wander. He was starting to have second thoughts about how he had handled the Johnson situation. It was a business decision. He had done what he had to do. She had left him no choice really. *No, that wasn't true.* Somehow she had come up with enough money to pay all the late fees and bring her account current. He hadn't expected that. He could have ended it right there. But he didn't. He still wanted her property, and he resented that she hadn't taken his advice.

McAfferty glanced at his watch. It was still early. He didn't need to get into the bank yet. In fact, he didn't feel like going in at all. He thought for a second. When was the last time he had taken a day off? He couldn't even remember—it had to be years. And what would happen if he didn't go in? Every one of his staff knew what to do. The bank would open up, his people would do their jobs, and business would go on just as usual. It really would make no difference if he went in or not.

McAfferty looked down the counter at Morretti and the others. He wondered if they ever felt like this. He wondered if they ever regretted their decisions and had second thoughts about the choices they had made in their lives? No, probably not, and neither should he. Second thoughts only caused problems. He had made his decision. He needed to stick with it and live with the consequences. McAfferty raised his hand to signal the waitress for a refill. No, he would go in today, but maybe he would go in late. That would shake everybody up.

Jodie, the big-boned red-haired waitress, came by and refilled his cup. He nodded at her and was about to take a sip when he heard a siren wailing. He turned around in his seat to look. Everyone else was looking out the big picture window too.

"Is that the fire truck?" Old Man Harris asked excitedly.

"No, they would have sounded the volunteer alarm first," said one of the Ganders brothers. "It might be the ambulance though."

"Uh-uh." Al Freely shook his head. "The ambulance goes whoop-whoop-dewhoop. This one's going whooooop-whoop-whooooop-whoop." He imitated the siren. "See? That's a patrol car."

"Are you sure?" Jim Baker chimed in. "I always thought the patrol cars sounded like Wu-wu-wu-whoooop. Wu-wu-wu-whoooop?"

"No, no. Maybe on TV, but that's not how they sound here," said Freely. "That's a patrol car."

The sound came closer. "I believe you're right, Al. That does sound like a patrol car," said Morretti.

"I've always had a good ear for those things," Freely said.

Then they were all off, chattering away about what might be going on and who had done what to whom. McAfferty turned back to the counter and took another sip of his coffee. There was almost no real crime in the whole county. The last time he'd heard a siren was a few months back when Agnes Peterson got her hand caught in a pickle jar.

This was probably something just as important.

The siren was screaming now, and McAfferty heard the

screech of rubber. He turned around again and watched the patrol car skid to a stop right in front of the diner. Then the siren stopped, the door flew open, and a patrolman stepped out. McAfferty shook his head. It was the crazy deputy, the one everyone called Stinky. McAfferty sighed. What a way to start the day.

The deputy charged through the door and weaved through the tables, straight for him. McAfferty's mouth dropped open in shock. It was not the way the man looked, with his wrinkled clothes, unshaven face, and bloodshot eyes. It was the money—twenty dollar bills. He clutched handfuls of them in both fists, and more money was stuffed down the front of his pants and sticking out from his pockets.

"I found it!" he shouted. "I found the money tree!"

"Wait a second," McAfferty said. "Calm down now."

"A money tree?" someone asked.

"That's impossible," someone else said. "There's no such thing."

McAfferty stood up. He had no idea what the deputy was talking about, but clearly he had found something out at the Johnson farm. The idea of a money tree was ridiculous, but whatever it was, it made no sense to talk about it in front of all these people. He reached out and grabbed the deputy's elbow. "Look, deputy, maybe we can talk about this back at my office."

Someone off to the side yelled out, "Where did you find it?"

"It's out at the Johnson farm!" The deputy spun toward the questioner, breaking McAfferty's grip. He was nearly beside himself with excitement. "I wouldn't have believed it if I hadn't seen it with my own eyes. It looks just like a regular tree, but instead of leaves, it has money!"

Everyone shouted out at the same time.

"Is it a real money tree?"

"Are you sure it's real?"

"The Johnsons have a money tree?"

"Look at this!" The deputy shook his hands in the air. "Yeah, it's real!"

"People, please," McAfferty put his hands in the air and raised his voice, trying to gain control. "Let's not get excited. I'm sure there's a reasonable explanation. There's no such thing as a money tree. Let me talk with the deputy alone, and I'll let you know what I find out."

"No way!" Al Freely kicked his chair back and pushed around the table to get to the door. "I'm heading out there to see this for myself."

"Me too!" Jim Baker shouted as he raced for the door.

"People wait!" McAfferty yelled. But it was too late. There was a mad dash for the door as everyone jumped up, knocking over chairs and tables as they rushed to get out.

"Stop!" McAfferty tried to stand in the way to slow them down, but the people pushed past him. In a matter of seconds, he was standing in the room alone. The street outside was alive with the sound of engines starting, tires squealing, and people yelling. The deputy took off again with his siren wailing. McAfferty shook his head.

The Deputy had blundered into something, and he supposed he should get out there to see what it was, but a money tree? That was too ridiculous to even contemplate. Then he heard a sound behind him. He looked back to see Jodie standing behind the counter, dialing the phone. He was about say how glad he was that not everyone had fallen for that nonsense about a money tree, when Jodie started talking excitedly into the phone.

"Bill? Drop what you're doing now, call my sister, and get yourself over to the Johnson's farm. They got a money tree!"

McAfferty pulled out his keys and headed for the door. It

seemed ridiculous, but if there was a real money tree, he wasn't going to be the last one to see it.

.30.

Grady

Grady had just finished breakfast, and was out doing his chores when he first heard the noise. It was a quiet, overcast day, and he was moving a little slow after being out so late at the concert. At first he thought it was cicadas or grasshoppers, but it didn't sound quite right. As the noise grew louder, it sounded more like a siren. He figured it was coming from down the road and getting closer. He ran toward the road to see what was going on. Luanne heard it too. She ran out of the house as he passed.

"What is it?" she asked.

"I don't know," Grady said. "But it's coming close."

They ran down the driveway and craned their necks to get a

better view. Grady was sure it was a siren now, and it was coming closer. And there was another sound, a deep rumbling. He nearly hopped up and down with excitement. Nothing ever happened down their way. In town, there was excitement all the time. But out here, they'd go days without talking to anyone but the mailman. With the siren wailing like that, this had to be big. A car chase maybe. Was the sheriff in hot pursuit of a gang of bank robbers? He wondered what he could do to help. If he had more time, he could try to make a road block. But the noise was so loud and so close now, he knew there wasn't time.

Then they rounded the corner and came into view. A police-car was in the front, its lights flashing, but there was a whole parade of cars and trucks behind it. And they were all going fast. Cars were weaving into the other lane like they couldn't wait to just follow the car in front of them. He'd never seen anything like it.

"Where are they going?" Luanne asked.

Grady shrugged his shoulders. There was nothing out here but farmland. He wondered if something had happened to the Cagles who had a farm farther down the road. He hoped it wasn't anything serious. They were an older couple and Ma said they were frail.

But as they came closer, he got the feeling they weren't going past them. They were heading right at them, going fast, swerving around, driving crazy. Grady and Luanne ran back to the big oak tree to get out of the way. They got there just in time. The police car pulled in first, its tires kicking up gravel, but the others were right behind. They swung in, one after the other. The first few took the driveway, but after that they cut over the grass, racing to get onto the Johnson's property.

The driveway quickly clogged with cars, but they kept coming. An old pick-up truck sped across the grass and hit the front fender of a newer Chevy. There was a crunch of metal. The Chevy owner leaned on his horn and there was some yelling. But it didn't last long because car doors were banging open and slamming shut as people jumped out of their cars and rushed forward. Grady recognized a lot of people from town, and even some neighbors. These were people who usually smiled at them and always acted friendly, but they ran past Grady and Luanne like they weren't even there.

The mob trampled the flower bed in the front yard and knocked over Luanne's new doll house. Luanne started crying and Grady couldn't do a thing about it. He didn't know what was happening. It felt scary to see people he knew and liked acting like this. People were running all over, and Grady and Luanne got swept along with them as they ran to the back of the house. Ma was back there, and Will too. Ma held her hands up and shouted for the people to stop, but no one did. Grady didn't know if they even heard her.

With the siren still going and all the other commotion, it was hard to even think.

Then someone shouted really loud, "It's over here!"

The crowd swarmed around the money tree. Some people were jumping up and grabbing leaves off the lower branches. Others climbed the tree and crawled out on the limbs trying to get the leaves off the higher branches. One of the Ganders brothers and Mrs. Holloway, Grady's old Sunday school teacher, were at the base of the tree, pushing and shoving each other, each one trying to get up first. Ma stood in front of the tree holding up her hands and shouting for people to stop. But they just pushed past her. People were rushing around, flailing their arms. It seemed that all they cared about was getting the money.

Luanne was crying hard now, and Grady felt tears coming to his eyes too. Something good had come into their lives. Now it was being destroyed. He wished he could do something, but he knew he couldn't. He wished he could just disappear, like he'd never been born at all. He saw Will standing off to the side all by himself, looking sadder than he'd ever seen a person look. Grady sniffed back the tears and clenched his fists. He wished Dad were here. He'd know what to do.

New people kept coming. The driveway and yard were packed, so they were driving in through the corn, running over and flattening it. Then a big pickup truck pulled in from the field. A large man in blue coveralls got out of the cab. He reached over and pulled a chainsaw out of the truck's bed. Grady didn't know the man, but his stomach fell as the man walked up to the tree.

"Move," the man yelled. "Get out of the way!"

Then he pulled the cord and the chainsaw started up with a roar. People moved away and dropped down from the tree as he began to cut. The engine whined. Wood chips and sawdust flew in the air, and it smelled like burning wood. After a few minutes, the tree began to tip. Everyone jumped back. The tree wobbled for a moment. Then it fell into the corn. It sounded like an explosion when it hit the ground. Everything got quiet for a moment. Then all the people jumped back in. Like flies on rotten meat, they covered the tree and stripped it bare.

There were others who couldn't get in close. They circled

around, looking for a place to jump in. Then someone yelled, "There's got to be more, let's look around!"

People ran in every direction. Some ran to the end of the property to check the trees there, others headed for the barn, and others headed for their house.

"I'll bet they keep the money in here!" someone shouted. A whole group of them charged into the barn.

Ma came over and hugged Grady and Luanne tight. Luanne buried her head in Ma's skirt and cried even harder.

"It's all right," Ma said as she stroked Luanne's hair. "It's going to be all right."

Grady knew she was wrong. Things were never going to be all right again. Ma always taught them to look for the good in people. She told them that most folks, deep down inside, were kind and decent. Grady looked around at all their neighbors, pushing and shoving, thinking about nothing but themselves, and he thought she was wrong about that too. Good people didn't act like this. Good people cared about others and tried their best to help people. Not like this. He didn't see how they could ever make things right again.

Someone finally turned the siren off. It seemed quieter, though it was still as crazy as before. People were still shouting, and

Grady heard the sound of clanging metal and breaking glass from inside the barn. They were throwing things out of both ends of the barn. He clenched his fists tighter. How much longer would they be here? He wanted everyone to finish whatever they were going to do and just leave. Then at least it would be quiet, and they'd be alone. The mob ran back and forth, throwing things out of the barn. It looked like they were going through everything, looking for money that wasn't there. They threw out the shelves and all the stuff that had been on them. They threw out all the boxes they'd had in there for storing things. It seemed like there wouldn't be anything left untouched by the time they were done. The heaps of stuff they'd gone through was piled high at both ends of the barn.

Then the sound started. At first it was so soft that Grady didn't even notice it. Then it got so loud that for a second he thought someone had flipped on the police car's alarm again. It was a sad sounding wail, and so loud it pierced his bones. When he figured out what it was, he turned around and looked at Will. Will was singing again. But now it wasn't for joy like he'd always sung before. It sounded like he was drowning in grief.

.31.

Ralwil Turth

After a while, the skies opened up and it started to rain. Ralwil could not even move. He stood motionless as the rain fell, soaking his clothes and turning the ground to mud. He watched as the last of the humans ran to their cars and drove away. After the money tree was down, and the barn was destroyed, and they hadn't found anything else, there was nothing to keep them there. They left with their heads down and their shoulders sagging. Ralwil looked around at the mess they had made. Big sections of the cornfield were flattened, and the grass was crisscrossed with deep ruts. The sweet-smelling flowers were ground into the dirt, and the air smelled foul from all the machines.

He turned toward the barn. The door hung from its hinges, and big piles of trash were heaped at both ends. Those piles of trash had been his chance to finish his repairs on the power drive and make his way back home. He had come so close. The composite had formed well, and he had enough to complete the core. But now it was all gone, mixed in with the broken shelves and debris, dissolving in the rain. Ralwil felt a lump in his throat. Then a pain shot through him, so bad it hurt to breathe. He gasped for breath and he recognized the emotion humans called grief.

Grady, Luanne, and the Ma stood close together, their arms circling each other, squeezing each other tight. He felt their sadness, and, for a moment, he thought about going over and joining them. But he could not. He was not one of them. They had brought him into their home, and for a while he had felt like he was part of their family grouping, but he knew he was not. They were humans and he was not. They acted different, they thought different, and no matter how much he tried he would never understand them. He was alone and different, and that was how it would be forever.

The pain spread in his stomach and he wondered what he could do now. With the composite machine ruined, and all the material he'd worked so long and hard on gone too, he was stuck—

stranded on this strange planet—with these creatures that he had no hope of ever understanding.

Ralwil felt moisture form in his eyes as he thought about all the things he would miss. He thought of the fresh smell of Quercia bushes after a rain, and the taste of morknfrut in the springtime. The sound of the ocean bells, and the way the rays of the red sun felt so soft against his outer membrane. All gone. He felt moisture run down his cheek as he thought about the glorious colors of the sunrise over the blue-green hills of his home city, and how he would never get to see them again. He thought of his swarm mates, and how much he would miss their connection, and how it physically hurt to know he would never experience it again. *Never.* For the first time since he had been on this planet, he truly understood the pain these humans felt.

When he reached up to wipe the moisture from his eyes, he saw that the Ma and her pups were staring at him, their eyes wide with shock. Ever since he first came to this planet and assumed this shape, people had stared at him, but this was not a look that the Ma and her brood normally assumed. As he wiped away his tears, he noticed his hand. It felt ticklish, as if it were pulsing, changing back and forth between his normal shape and this human appearance he had taken on.

That meant the pod's battery was failing. The last of the reserve power was nearly gone.

.32.

Grady

Looking back on it, Grady and his family knew something was different about Will right from the start. He'd never seemed normal, but they'd explained it away, figuring that was just the way he was. Everybody is different in some ways, and they didn't have much experience with people outside of the ones they knew. But after the money tree came, it must have crossed their minds that Will had something to do with it. No other explanation made any sense. It's easy to look back at things *after* they've happened and come up with all sorts of reasons for why they happened. But when something's happening, you're so caught up in the moment that things don't seem so obvious.

Will stood in front of them, only it wasn't Will, and it was, all at the same time. Grady thought he looked like one of those 3D cards they sometimes have in cereal boxes, where it looks like one thing from one angle, and something entirely different from another. Part of him was Will, the other part was something Grady had never seen before, a creature of some kind. It was small, shorter than Luanne, only a few feet high at the most. Its skin was purplish-blue, and it looked slick like it was wet. The body was lumpy, and if it had a head, he couldn't tell where it was. There were no eyes or nose, or even a mouth, as far as he could see. The creature that had been Will had arms and legs of a sort, but they looked nothing like what he thought of as arms and legs. They looked more like the tentacles on an octopus, thin and rubbery looking. His legs were coiled down and folded beneath him for support. The thing was ugly and weird, and Grady thought they should have been scared, but they weren't—or he wasn't, anyway. This was still Will, and in a way, Grady had known all along that he wasn't who he appeared to be.

Ma squeezed them tighter, and Grady felt her tremble. He was so mixed up. Just moments before, it seemed like his life was over and everything they'd had was lost. Now, more than sadness, he was shocked. He was seeing something that had to be impossible, but he knew it was real. Will looked like a scary creature not of this earth. He wasn't who Grady thought he was, but he'd been his friend.

The part that was Will faded out as the part that was the monster grew stronger. Right before Will faded away completely, Grady looked in his eyes, and saw how afraid he was. Grady stared at him and knew that as bad as things were for them, somehow they were even worse for Will. Looking at him, even though Grady knew he wasn't human, he knew what Will was feeling. He knew the pain and the loss. He knew the pain because he'd felt it before, and he'd seen the same look before. Will's eyes looked like Ma's eyes, right after Dad died.

And then the last bit of Will faded, and he was gone.

"I think he's scared," Luanne said.

The rain fell harder. They all stood for another moment, hugging each other tight as they stared at the creature. Ma squeezed them again tightly and Grady squeezed back. Then he broke away and took a step forward, toward the creature that had once been Will.

"I think he needs our help," he said.

.33.

Ralwil Turth

The rain felt hard and cold against Ralwil's skin. He had loved the climate here before; now it seemed harsh and inhospitable. How could he survive here? How could he live among these creatures who took what was meant for good and destroyed it? How could he live in a world where he was alone and unprotected? He wondered what would happen next. Now that the family knew who he really was, he couldn't pretend anymore. The family had treated him as if he was of their brood before, but now they looked at him with fear and disgust. He would have to move off the farm and find some other way to live.

Soon the town's inhabitants would learn who he really was.

What would happen then? He knew they looked at him as strange and out of place when he was in human form. They were afraid of him. How would they see him now? Ralwil knew the answer.

He was something to be destroyed.

Before, when he was sure he would get back home, this seemed like a great adventure. It was hope that gave him energy and the will to move on. That was all gone. How could he live here on this hostile planet? He could not. Ralwil slumped down as he felt his very life force begin to fade.

.34.

Grady

Grady closed his eyes and took a step forward. His hands shook and his legs felt wobbly. He realized that he was scared after all. He took another step, but it didn't feel like he was walking. More like he was floating and he wasn't in control of his own body. This felt like a dream. There were no such things as space aliens – that was impossible. Just like there were no such things as trees that grew money. But this seemed so real, and if it was a dream, then everything was a dream, going all the way back before Dad died. Could he still wake up in his bed and find that everything was back the way it was before?

He closed his eyes and tried to stay calm. It felt like the

whole world had crashed down on them today. The money tree was gone, Will was gone, and everything seemed darker. The world was suddenly a scary place and he didn't know what he could do to change that. Grady was just a few steps away from Ma and Luanne, but all of a sudden he felt frightened and alone. He couldn't stop the people who had ruined their farm, even though he tried. He couldn't help Ma when she needed him most, and he was too scared of what Will really was to even look at him. He felt like running away. He was afraid he was going to start crying.

Grady took a deep breath and opened his eyes. He had to be strong. The creature in front of him had no eyes or nose or anything resembling a face. It stood still, not making even a sound. But this wasn't a creature—this was Will, his friend. Even though he looked scary and he wasn't who Grady had thought he was, this was still Will. Somehow he knew Will was in pain. Grady didn't know what he could do to help, but he had to try.

He pushed back his fear and moved another step forward.

.35.

Ralwil Turth

The ticklish sensation in his body stopped, and Ralwil Turth knew that he had fully returned to his natural form. After so long in a human body, it felt strange to be back in his own. He felt too close to the ground and too exposed. Grady, the Ma, and Luanne stared at him. They finally saw him for who he really was, and he knew that they were frightened. If only he had stayed in his pod and concentrated on fixing the power source. He had failed. He had failed in fixing his drive. He had failed in keeping his true form a secret from the inhabitants of this planet. And he had failed when he'd tried to help the family grouping. Everything he'd tried had turned out terribly wrong.

Ralwil looked at the Ma. Now that she saw him for who he was, she would surely come forward to protect her brood. He didn't blame her. Seeing him like this, she had to think he was a threat. It was only natural. He wished he could talk with her and try to explain. But outside his human form, he didn't have vocal cords, so there was no way to speak. Well, if she was going to attack, so be it. He had never expected it to end like this, but at least it would all be over and he wouldn't have to worry any more about how he could ever manage to survive on this strange, alien planet. He blurred his vision sensors and waited for her to strike.

Grady moved forward slowly. He stopped for a moment, then moved forward again. He stood close, only a few feet away, with his hands stretched out and his palms up. This was the boy he had grown so close to, but he could tell that Grady saw him differently now. Still, he didn't fear Grady like he did the Ma. From what he had learned of human expressions, he knew the boy was very afraid. Ralwil lifted an arm and hesitantly reached forward. He realized Grady was speaking, his voice low, almost drowned out by the rain. "It's okay, Will. It's okay." His voice seemed to shake. Grady took another step, his hand extended.

The boy was still trying to connect with him. Even after

seeing him for who he really was, he still wanted to make contact. Ralwil saw the fear in his eyes, but there was something else. Ralwil's darkness faded for a moment as he looked into Grady's eyes. As bad as he felt now, his time on this planet had meant something, and much of this was because of this boy. He could not talk with him, but he could connect again through a synch-link. Ralwil tried to relax, then sent off a soft, welcoming wave as he synched in with Grady's mind.

It took hold almost at once, and the images and feelings flowed. He was back in the family house, only it looked different now. The ceiling towered above him so it looked as high as the sky. The furniture was meant for giants. Everything seemed so big. But the world was so big because he was so small. He felt the carpet on his hands and his knees. He reached out to a small table to pull himself up. Then he let go of the table and balanced on his own legs. This was a new and wonderful feeling. He teetered back and forth, in awe of his accomplishment.

"Good job, Grady. Now come here."

The voice came from off to the side. It was a man, tall and strong, with bright blue eyes and a big smile on his face. He knew at once that this was Da, his father. Da sat on the floor with his arms outstretched. Ralwil, as Grady, turned toward him, took a hesitant step forward, and immediately toppled, landing on his behind with a thump. The shock only lasted an instant though. He pulled himself back up and stood again.

"That's it, Grady. You can do it."

Ralwil took another step, wobbled, and fell back again. But it didn't matter if he fell. He would try again, and again and again if it took another thousand tries. He had to walk, to move on his own, and he would keep trying until he could. And all at once he *was* walking, standing upright, moving along with ease. Then in an instant he was running through the house as fast as he could move, laughing as his Da chased after him in play.

"I'm going to get you Buddy, I'm going to get you."

Ralwil felt himself scooped up from behind, lifted into the air and placed on his Da's shoulders. He laughed with joy. It was so high up here, he was on top of the world. They walked through the house with his Da holding his ankles, Ralwil's legs wrapped around his neck. Then Da ducked low as they went through the doorway and outside into the bright sunlight. Ralwil squealed with pleasure as they ran outside. The colors were intense, the sky so blue and the grass so green. This whole world seemed brand new. Ma was there too, and soon he was between them, hugged tight from both sides. He felt safe and protected and loved. He was at the center of the world.

Then he was bigger, though still not big. His world had expanded now and his domain spread throughout the house to the front yard and back to the barn. Now he was outside again with his Da. No, it wasn't Da, now it was Dad, and they were underneath the big oak tree in the front yard. They looked down at the ground as a baby bird struggled to stand up.

"Can't we help it, Dad?"

Dad bent down on one knee and studied the creature. "Its leg is broken, son. His Mama can't help him and there's not a lot we can do. I don't think he's going to make it."

Ralwil felt the sadness well up and tears filled his eyes. It was no fair, the little bird didn't do anything wrong. Why did it have to die?

Dad put an arm around his shoulders. "I know, son. It hurts to see little things suffer."

"But Dad, you can fix anything."

And he did. Dad put a splint on the leg and together they took care of the little bird, feeding it and nursing it to health. Ralwil watched the little bird and saw it take over a section of the work-bench in the barn as if it was his own nest. The leg healed and soon it was hopping along the bench with excitement every time they came into the barn. He watched as the bird became a normal part of their lives until one day it just flew away, never to return. Ralwil felt a mix of sadness and pride that he had helped the small creature live.

More images and emotions washed over his mind. Luanne was now in the family and it felt like his parents love was split in two. He resented the baby and wanted life back like it was before. But this didn't last. He found his parents' love was boundless. They could love the new baby without loving him any less. Quick flashes of joy and laughter flowed through his mind. Christmas, unwrapping presents, music and snow, and the anticipation that made the whole season magical. Sledding down a high hill and feeling the cold and the wind in his face, feeling like he was flying. And then it was springtime. The world was reborn. He found tadpoles in a puddle behind the barn. More memories and emotions flowed. He was older now and had friends and his own dreams and secrets. Ma was all about love. Dad was the man he wanted to become when he grew up. But his world was wider now, and his parents were only part of this world.

Then the scene shifted and it was nighttime. He was inside the warm house, lying on the living room floor next to Luanne, reading a book. He heard car tires crunching down on their gravel driveway. It was Dad, home from his business in town. He kept on reading, waiting for Dad to walk in the door. Then the doorbell rang. This was strange. No one came out here this late at night. He jumped up to see who it was. Ma was already at the door. Ralwil stood behind her as she opened it. The Sheriff stood at the doorstep, holding his hat in his hands.

"I'm sorry, Helen," he said. "I don't know how to tell you this, but there's been an accident."

Then Ma was crying and Luanne was bawling and the Sheriff didn't know what to do. Ralwil couldn't breathe. It felt like his whole body was being squeezed from all sides. His heart thumped wildly against his chest and he felt weak. He stood as still as a rock in shocked silence. This couldn't be real, but he knew that it was. Dad was the strongest, the bravest, the best. How could this happen to him?

Quick flashes of hope for the future and Ma's love passed through his mind, but Ralwil pulled back and felt the darkness close in on him. This was still a wound for Grady, not fresh but not healed over. What kind of world was this? If the good and the strong like Dad couldn't survive, how could he? He wished he believed that somehow things could turn out better, but he didn't see it and he didn't feel it. The world seemed so dark that he didn't think such a thing as hope could even exist.

He understood Grady better. Now he truly understood what they called grief. He was trapped on a cruel, cold world. Maybe Grady and his family would survive, but he could not. This he knew for sure. The grief would kill him. Ralwil felt a sharp pain as the images slipped away. His body slumped as his life energy faded.

.36.

Grady

Grady had never dreamed of a world like this. He stood in a grove of tall purple plants with rectangular shaped orange and yellow fruit that hung like mobiles, swaying in the breeze—*Kordoon*, they called it. The taste reminded him of shoe polish and motor oil, but in a good way. The air smelled sweet, almost like it was scented with cinnamon. Even the sun felt different. But then the sun *was* different. Though the star was high in the sky, its red rays painted the world in a sunset-like haze. The air felt cool and nicely dry, and though everything was strange and new, it all felt comforting and familiar.

The creatures—they called themselves the *Schle-hhnk*—were

a wonder to behold. Small and grotesque looking, yet oddly attractive, they moved through large cities that looked like anthills, bumping into each other and crawling over one another, in a way that appeared disorganized and random, but was really more like a dance, beautiful and precise in its movements. This was the swarm, the time when all the Schle-hhnk born in a particular moon cycle returned to their home city and spent a mourlong together, linking their brains in a communal frenzy of joy and experience sharing.

This all felt like a dream, and yet at the same time so real. Grady realized that this was happening to him. Somehow his mind had linked in with Will's and Will was showing him his world, the way that he knew it.

For the first time Grady knew his real name. Though he had been calling him Will, his real name was Ralwil Turth. He was an Interplanetary Engineer of the Primary Class from the house of Turth, one of the best pedigrees on his planet. This planet was his home and he thought of it often, though he had not been there in ages.

Then the images changed and Grady was alone on a small craft in deep space. He was on his own for months on end, and he felt the isolation, but also an exhilarating sense of mission. He was doing something new and important. Grady smelled a whiff of something foul and he felt like gagging. It smelled like rotting garbage, thick and ripe, so strong it was hard to breathe. Then he saw a creature that looked something like a cross between a butterfly and an evergreen tree, and he knew that this was the source of the wretched smell. Its name was FyyrsyyytG.g, and despite the smell, it was one of the sweetest, most caring souls Ralwil had ever come across. They had served together in close quarters for over a year on an exploration of a mineral rich moon in the Phornos system. By the end, Ralwil had learned to appreciate everything about his friend, smell and all.

Images flashed across Grady's mind. He saw all sorts of amazing creatures. Some looked like bugs, others seemed almost human, others didn't seem like anything he'd ever seen or could even dream of. Life, intelligent life, was common. Throughout the known universe, thousands of intelligent species had been identified and categorized. Most of them had been brought into the Universal Whole long ago.

Civilization, interplanetary civilization, was older than anyone knew.

New memories came into his mind. Grady, as Ralwil, was

back in the pod, shooting through space, on his way home. Just the thought of touching down on his home planet, breathing the sweet air and touching minds with his swarm mates, gave him a pleasant glow. He was eager to be home again, but wondering how things had changed.

What would he do first? Visit his birthplace and show respect to his elders? Maybe take a trip to the coastal shore to wade into the shallow water and feel the warmth of the Xyqrel ocean? Or go to the mountains to listen to the song of the Qsertegols? So many things he could do, so many pleasures to experience.

Then, without warning, the lights in the pod flashed. The power source was out. He had to make a decision fast, while there was still some reserve power left. He had no other options, so the decision was easy. The pod rocketed toward a water-based planet, using up the last of its power. He felt a smack of terror as the pod hit the atmosphere and it felt like his skelfones would shake loose from his skin. Then, with a jolt, he was on the ground. Safe, at least for now.

Grady saw the farm through Ralwil's eyes. The fields that he had grown up with and taken for granted, looked at as ordinary and common, now seemed exotic and new. He saw himself and his family from Ralwil's perspective, and he realized how frightening it was to be alone and so far from home. But he had a plan, a plan for how to fix the power source and make his way home. Equations and chemical symbols flooded his mind. Long formulas with strange symbols now seemed as clear to him as words on a page. Everything he needed to fix the drive was right here on the farm. All he needed were the right supplies and a little time. He had a plan, but he hadn't counted on being drawn in by these humans. Images of the money tree ran through his mind, how it grew from a thought, to a twig, to a towering growth, its leaves unfurled and ripe with promise.

This was going to be the answer, the solution to all the family grouping's problems. But it was not. It only made things worse.

Grady watched again as all the townspeople rushed around the farm, crazy with greed, destroying everything they came across. He saw how the people were breaking things in the barn and throwing them all out into a pile—all the things needed to fix the power supply. How they upended the composite tubs and trampled everything into the dirt. Suddenly it hit him. All his weeks of work were undone in just a few minutes. Any chance of fixing the power supply and getting off this planet was now gone. A deep blackness settled over him. How could he even survive? It was hard to breathe, hard to think.

How would he survive?

Over these last long months since Dad died, Grady sometimes felt low and there was a darkness too, but never as deep as this. He pulled back and all at once the connection was broken. He hung his head, grasping his knees as he tried to catch his breath. The rain had soaked his clothes and plastered his hair against his face. But he was himself again. His head was cloudy and his whole body felt weak. Somehow he had been inside another creature's mind, seeing things the way that Will did. What an amazing life he had. But the darkness . . .

Grady couldn't let go of the last thought. There was no hope. No possibility of hope. *How could he go on?* And he knew that he couldn't—not by himself. Somehow it dawned on him, Will was not just down, he was dying!

Then another thought came to Grady in a flash. *He could help*!

Yes, but how? He closed his eyes again and tried to remember what he had seen. He had to help Will fix his spacecraft. Somehow there was a solution. It was something so simple, and it was right in front of his face. The symbols and equations flashed in his mind again, and he saw them clearly and understood what they meant. All at once it was clear. Will had thought that corn was the solution. But it wasn't corn that formed the composite.

Grady stood up straight, took a deep breath, and felt energy flow back into his body. He looked at the creature he now knew as Ralwil Turth, though he still thought of him as Will. He wanted to let him know that he was going to help him, but the connection was gone. Grady turned back to Ma and Luanne. They stared back at him in wide-eyed concern.

"It's sugar!" he said.

.37.

Ralwil Turth

Ralwil felt his energy fade as blackness surrounded him. His body turned slack and he slid toward the ground. It took too much effort to resist, so he didn't even try. He let his body disengage from his mind. He had failed in his mission. There was no reason to go on.

The darkness closed in on him like water. He could hardly breathe. It felt like he was drowning.

The darkness closed in tighter.

.38.

Grady

Grady didn't know what happened, but somehow he had changed. He wasn't just a kid any more—or at least he didn't feel that way. Will was in trouble and Grady knew that he was the only person who could save him.

"Grady, are you okay?" He could hear the concern in Ma's voice.

"I'm okay, Ma," he said. "I know what to do. It's sugar! We can use sugar to form the composite to fix Will's power drive. "

They both just stared at him like he was speaking another language, and maybe he was. He still saw flashes of Ralwil's world. Somehow that world and Will's memories were part of him now. He wanted to tell them all about it, tell them how Will had really gotten here and what he had seen and felt. How he understood Will now, he knew who Will really was and he loved him all the more because of it. But there was no way he could explain it to them. He didn't have time to try anyway. Grady knew Will was dying and he had to save his friend.

"Luanne," he commanded, "run up to the house and bring all the sugar you can find. Anything sweet, honey, syrup, bring that too."

Luanne didn't hesitate. She sprinted back toward the house.

"Ma," he said, "we need to get Will down to the barn and see what we can save from the composite."

"Grady, I don't . . . "

"I'll try to explain later, Ma. We don't have time now. I think Will is dying."

Ma nodded. Looking into her eyes, Grady saw the fear and the uncertainty, but he also knew she would do anything to help Will.

Will slumped down further. Grady could tell he was slipping away. He didn't look like he could move on his own. Without another word, Ma walked over and put her arm around Will. Grady put his arm around from the other side. Together, moving slowly, almost carrying him, they walked to the barn.

The rain had slowed now, but the ground was muddy and puddles of water collected in the tracks where the cars had been. The front of the barn was littered with all the stuff the mob had thrown out, and there was a big pile of trash near the entrance. Chunks of wood and parts of broken shelving were mixed in with the tubes and cans and broken parts of Will's machine. There was broken glass and twisted metal.

Mixed in with all this were bluish things that looked like pieces of broken dinner plates. They set Will down by the side of the barn. Then Grady carefully pulled out one of the bluish pieces. It smelled vaguely like burnt sugar. He lifted it to his mouth and stuck out his tongue.

"Grady!" Ma called out.

"It's okay, Ma," he said. "This is what Will was making. I need to make sure I've got this right." He licked it. It was sweet, and definitely sugar like, but there was something else here too. This wasn't sugar, but it was close enough. He grabbed one of the big metal tubs Will had been using and tossed the bluish piece into the tub.

"Ma, we need to collect as much of this as we can. We don't have much time!"

It was still drizzling, but they were already about as wet as they could get, so it didn't really matter anymore. Ma picked up a piece of the bluish stuff, glanced at it for a second, then dropped it in the tub on top of the other piece. Grady dug in, looking for more. There were lots of sharp edges, rough wood, and broken glass, so they had to be careful. Usually Ma would have made Grady go find gloves, but today she didn't say a thing.

Grady looked over at Will—he thought of him as Will again, even though he looked so different. He was slumped over. He had seemed short when he'd first changed into the creature, but now he seemed even shorter, as if he was shrinking. Together Grady and Ma worked fast, carefully moving things around looking for blue pieces. In a few minutes they had filled up most of the tub.

Luanne ran back with a pillowcase slung over her shoulder. "There's more. I couldn't carry it all."

She dumped out the pillowcase. There were three big bags of sugar and a jar of home made syrup.

She picked up the empty pillowcase and ran back to the house. "I'll be right back," she called.

Grady dumped the sugar and poured the syrup in with the bluish chunks of composite. *Now what?* he wondered. He wasn't sure what to do next. Ma was over by Will and she looked worried. Will's long strange looking arms hung limply by his side.

He seemed to be melting into himself.

"What do we do now, Grady?" Ma asked.

Grady closed his eyes and thought. They needed this to fix the spaceship, so they needed to get to where it was. Maybe if Will were by his pod he would feel better.

"We need the wheelbarrow," he said. "We need to get all this down by the creek where his pod is."

Grady ran back into the barn, slipping around in the mud as he ran. The wheelbarrow was upside down with one handle leaning against the side wall where someone had tossed it. He right-sided it and pushed it out through the mud as fast as he could. Then Ma helped him put the big tub into the wheelbarrow.

Luanne came back with more sugar and they added this to the tub. The mixture of the bluish composite, the sugar, the syrup, and rainwater looked like nothing but a big mess. He hoped he was doing the right thing.

Grady picked up the handles on the wheelbarrow and tried

to push. He strained against it, but the wheel sank in the mud and it hardly moved. Ma grabbed hold of one handle and Grady took the other. They both pushed, and together they got it too budge. It felt awkward and it was hard to keep steady, but once they got it moving, it went pretty well. They steered it down the path, past the barn and along the cornfield toward the creek. After a while they stopped for a second to catch their breath, and he looked back. Luanne was following behind them with Will, walking slowly, her arms around him, carrying him like a baby.

Ma picked up the handle and they started again. The ground was a little soggy, but the thick grass kept it from getting muddy, so they were able to move along faster than before. They they reached the creek, and even though he knew it would be there, Grady's mouth dropped open.

He didn't know how many times he'd been back here over the summer, but he'd come down this way nearly every day. He could have made a map of this area showing every tree, rock, and bush, just from memory. But standing right there, in the weeds by the creek, was a strange orange metal thing that looked like a rounded-off football. The sky and the trees were reflected in it like a mirror. Grady knew this was Will's spaceship. He had seen it clearly when their minds were linked. But he couldn't figure out how he could have missed it being here all this time.

They pushed the wheelbarrow around the bend to the spaceship. Grady couldn't stop staring at it. He wondered how it worked and what it looked like inside. They set the wheelbarrow down close to it. He looked into the tub. What to do now? He couldn't see how the mess in the tub was going to help Will or get his spaceship working again.

He looked back to see how Will was doing, It seemed like he'd shrunk down even smaller. Luanne still had her arms around him, but he was sagging like his whole body had turned to jelly. Grady rushed over and put his arm around Will's other side. It felt strange to touch him. His skin was cool and rubbery. Grady tried to boost him up, but Will kept sagging.

"Come on, Will," he said. "You're going to be okay."

"Come on, Will," Luanne cried. "Don't give up!"

Grady didn't know if he could hear them or not. Will slumped forward. He seemed to be getting worse by the second. His body flopped against the ground. Even with Luanne and Grady holding him up the best they could, Will was still as limp as a dead worm. Grady's heart raced faster. He was afraid they were too late.

.39.

Ralwil Turth

The world was dark and he felt so tired. Too tired to support himself. Too tired to think. Too tired to even breathe.

Without hope, why go on?

What was left to live for? Lost and so very far from home, without any hope of ever seeing his swarm mates again, Ralwil let go. The string that held his being together snapped and his body sank down to merge with the earth. Just let go and wait for the pain and grief to stop. Down, down, down till there was nothing. And then he felt like he was floating.

Gravity didn't weigh him down anymore. Now he was as light as foam. A bubble of air floating up toward the surface of a pond. As he floated upward, a feeling of warmth and peacefulness flowed across his body. He realized he was dying, but he did not mind. There were things he still wanted to do with his life, but they didn't matter anymore. He had lived a full life. He'd seen so much more of the universe than his swarm mates could even imagine. He wished he had made it back to share his experiences with them. But that was how life worked. No regrets. He floated higher.

He rose more quickly now. His mind filled with colors, scents, tastes, and sounds. All the experiences of his life came back to him like a synch-link in overdrive. The tastes of watermelon and qwezdel juice. The sounds of the Elden wind, church bells, and surf. The scents of gortwig, cinnamon, and methane. The cold chill of deep space. His mind flooded with experiences. He absorbed them like a sponge, and floated higher. Such bliss.

He sensed that he was up nearly as far as he could go. At some point the bubble would pop and he would be transformed. He settled into his bliss and waited for what would happen next.

Then he heard a voice. A human voice calling to him, though it sounded no louder than a whisper. For a second he felt the bliss dissolve.

NO. He couldn't go back. Going back meant a return of grief and more pain.

He let go again. The sound faded as he returned to his bubble, blanketed by the bliss.

.40.

Grady

"Please, God, don't let him die." Luanne held the tiny alien in her arms like a broken doll. "Will," she called. "Will, wake up, Will."

Tears ran down her cheeks and Grady felt himself choking up too. This wasn't fair. Why did Will have to die? He had done nothing but try to help. Luanne was sobbing and Grady felt his tears start to flow too.

Luanne called his name over and over again. "Will. Will. Will."

Grady wiped his eyes and tried to think. There had to be something he could do. He was the only one who could help. But he had no idea what to do next. If he did nothing, Will would die. He closed his eyes and tried to get an image of what to do, but nothing came. Will had started sinking when his plans for getting back home were gone. Grady *had* to find a way for Will to get back home. He was so sure that sugar was the answer to making Will's composite, but the mess in the tub didn't look like anything you would put in that shiny spaceship. He squeezed his eyes tight and tried to remember what the composite was supposed to look like. He saw an image of crystals that looked almost like pellets. All at once he felt that he was still on the right track. But he was missing something. What?

Back in the barn, Will had bubbling pots and tubes that moved things around. He'd been taking one thing and changing it into something entirely new. Grady thought of how they'd sat around the campfire eating the s'mores, and how the heat had transformed the marshmallows into something different. Even when Ma cooked, she transformed food from one thing into something else. Heat changed things, but that would take time. A thought came to him: Electricity. He didn't know what made him think of it, but at once he knew it was right.

"Come back, Will," Luanne cried.

Grady didn't have time to wait. He eased away from Will,

leaving Luanne to cradle him closer, and ran for the barn.

"Grady, where are you going?"

"I'll be back, Ma," he called. "We don't have much time."

He sprinted into the barn. Both the front and back doors were open, so he could see well enough just from the outside light. He took a second to look around and caught his breath. The place was a mess. All the things that had been on the workbench were knocked off and scattered on the ground. The floor was covered with pieces of wood and broken glass. It looked like there'd been an earthquake or something. It was hard to believe their neighbors had done this. He walked slowly, being careful where he stepped, over to where the workbench had been.

Dad always kept the extension cords, along with some of his small power tools, in a big wooden box underneath the workbench. The box was gone, but the extension cords, all bright orange, were heaped on the ground nearby.

He picked up the whole pile of cords and headed toward the back door. He wanted to run, but he had to be careful moving through the mess and it was hard to see with his arms loaded up with the extension cords. He found an outlet near the back door and plugged a cord into it. He looped the cord around a pole so it wouldn't come unplugged if he accidentally pulled too hard. Then he walked out the back door and through the pen, ducked under the fence bottom, and trotted down toward the creek. A few more yards was as long as the first cord would reach. He untangled the second cord and made a knot in the ends, the way his dad had shown him, so it wouldn't unplug when he pulled on it. He linked it into the first. Then he went on as far as the next cord would reach and linked up the third cord.

He worked as fast as he could, but it seemed to take forever. He came to the end of the field with the fifth cord, the last one he had. Ma and Luanne were on the ground in front of the spaceship, holding Will. Luanne was sobbing. Grady had a bad feeling about what was happening. He didn't know what he would do if Will died on them. He fought back tears as he hurried forward.

The fifth cord was just long enough to get to the spot where they were waiting. Ma stood up. Her eyes were wet and Grady knew she'd been crying too. She looked at him and the extension cords, then over at the tub. She knew what he was going to do. She nodded her head.

"Be careful," she said.

He took the end of the cord like it was a live snake, then

tossed it into the vat of liquid. This seemed crazy. The cord made a snapping sound as it hit the surface. Then a big blue spark rose above it. Almost instantly, the liquid started to boil. Big thick bubbles rose and popped so quickly, it sounded like popcorn. The air was filled with that sweet, sweet cotton candy smell, mixed with a sharper, harsher smell. But this went on for only a few seconds. Then the popcorn sound sped up so fast that it blended into one long sound. Then it stopped. Standing back, Grady peeked over the rim of the tub. All the liquid was gone. The tub was filled with small white crystals. They almost looked like dull diamonds.

His plan had somehow worked. These pellets were like those he had seen when his mind was connected to Will's. He looked at Will. Ma was crouched beside him and Luanne still had her arms around him, saying his name over and over.

The composite was ready. Will could go home now. Only he didn't move. He lay there as still as before. Grady knelt down in the mud and put his hands on Will's cold, stiff body.

Suddenly he realized, they were too late. Will wasn't dying. He was dead. All they'd done to try and save him didn't matter. Will was gone.

Grady broke down sobbing, and, like Luanne, saying Will's

name over and over again.

"Will," he cried. "I'm sorry, Will."

Ma put her arms around them. Grady knew she felt just as low as he did. The world felt dark again. Dad had died, and now Will was dead too. The future seemed bleak. What would they do now? It felt like the night when the Sheriff came to tell them Dad had died.

Then he felt something. He felt Will twitch.

.41.

Ralwil Turth

Ralwil floated higher, but now there was a crack in his bubble of bliss. He heard his name being called, again and again. He tried to let go, but the intruding voices kept calling him.

Stop it!

He wanted to go back to the peace and the solitude, back to his memories and the joy of what was about to happen. But the voices wouldn't stop. It felt like they were trying to pull him out of his bubble. Ralwil fought against the voices, but he couldn't help hearing them, and each time he heard his name took him further from the bliss. He wasn't falling, but his bubble was no longer rising.

He turned enough to face the sound, and all at once he recognized it. It was a human voice, the voice of the youngest pup, Luanne. Then he realized there was another voice, and it was Grady's. His bliss moved farther away. They were calling to him, and he could sense their sadness. He listened again and felt their pain. Their grief. And it was all for him.

They were grieving HIM.

Ralwil felt his bubble start to drop. The family grouping had been through so much, and now he had caused them more sadness. They had given him love and he had repaid them with pain. The voices sounded closer. He had learned about human love from them. Even when they saw him as he really was, they still showed him love.

He couldn't cause them more pain.

His bubble cracked open and he began to fall. But the fall did not scare him. He felt the love flow stronger and he felt his energy grow. Then, in the space of a breath, he was back on the ground. The family grouping was all there, and he could sense their joy. He sat up and took a deep breath of the earth air. He smelled the distinct aroma of the power unit. Somehow it had worked.

He was going home.

.42.

Grady

Grady didn't know how it happened, but one second Will was dead, or at least they thought he was, and the next he was standing up and moving around like nothing had happened. Luanne squealed with pleasure. She grabbed Grady and pulled him into a big hug. Grady felt like dancing, he was so happy.

Making a strange gurgling sound, Will waddled toward the wheelbarrow. Grady thought he was sniffing the air. Then, when he was almost next to the wheelbarrow, he touched something on his belt and a big spark flew to the tub. It made a crackling noise and the air smelled like it did after a thunder shower. Then Will started to change, flipping back and forth between the Will they knew and the creature that was really Will. After a second the change stopped, and it was Will standing there the way they'd known him, as big and strong as ever.

He looked down at them and smiled. "Thank you," he said to Ma in his slow, deep voice.

Then he touched something on his belt, and a hole slid open in the side of the spaceship. Will picked up the tub from the wheelbarrow as if it were a ball of cotton. He carried it the few steps to the spaceship, tilted it through the opening in the ship, and poured the contents inside. He shook the last of the crystals out before pulling the tub away and placing it gently back in the wheelbarrow. Will pushed another button on his belt and the opening in the spaceship silently closed again.

After a second Grady heard a low humming sound and felt a vibration that started from the ground and made his knees shake. Will had his eyes closed and a big smile on his face. The vibration grew stronger until Grady's whole body was shaking. He was sure he was going to fall down. Was this what an earthquake felt like?

Then the noise and the vibration stopped just as quickly as they had begun. The air was still. The only sound was leaves rustling in the wind. Even the crickets were quiet. Will touched another button on his belt, and without a sound, another hole opened in the side of the spaceship. A ramp eased itself out of the ship and onto the ground. Grady tried to look inside the ship, but it was dark and he couldn't see much of anything. There didn't seem to be enough room for anyone to live in, even someone as small as Will would be when he turned back into the creature.

Will's smile disappeared. Grady wasn't sure, but he thought he saw a tear in his eye. "I . . . I go now," Will said.

They all rushed forward and hugged him. Luanne was crying, and Grady was too, but he wasn't sad. He was crying mostly because he felt so happy. Then they let him go and Will stepped to the bottom of the ramp. He looked like he was going to try to walk right inside, and as big as he was, there was no way he was going to fit. But then he turned back toward the family, opened his mouth wide, and began to sing. His voice sounded like a mix between a fog horn and a fire alarm. The song didn't have much of a tune, but Grady felt the vibrations flow across his body. It made him smile. He was glad they had a chance to hear him sing one last time.

When Will stopped singing, he waved. Then he touched a button on his belt again, and they watched as he shifted shape. Will disappeared and the alien creature stood in his place. He waved once more with his tentacle-like arm, then turned around and wobbled up the ramp. The doors slid shut as soon as he went inside.

The family all stepped back waiting for the engines to go on. After the earthquake vibrations they'd felt before, Grady was sure this would be a spectacular liftoff. But without a sound or warning of any kind, the ship began to rise, floating up above the ground like a helium balloon. It rose up, higher and higher, until they had to tilt their necks all the way back just to see it. When it was high in the sky, it paused and rocked backwards once, then forward, almost like it was waving. Then, in the blink of an eye, it shot up toward the clouds and disappeared from view.

Grady, Luanne, and Ma stood looking up at the spot where the pod had been. Luanne laughed. Then Grady laughed too. Then Ma was laughing as hard as he'd ever seen her laugh. They just felt so filled with joy that they couldn't hold it in. And Grady knew right then, even with all the troubles they had, even though they might have more troubles as time went on, they were going to be all right. No matter what happened around them, they were going to be together, and somehow they'd get through.

Grady linked arms with Ma on one side and Luanne on the other. They turned back toward the house, but suddenly they stopped. Standing behind them, not more than twenty steps back, stood Mr. McAfferty from the bank.

Grady didn't know how long he'd been standing there, but from the glazed look in his eyes and the way his mouth hung open, he could tell he'd been there long enough to see what had just happened. They all stood still for a moment. Then, without saying a word, Ma stepped right up to Mr. McAfferty. She looked into his eyes. It almost seemed like she felt sorry for him. With all the money and power he had, he really didn't have that much after all. Grady and his family had each other, and they were richer than he would ever be.

Ma walked past Mr. McAfferty, and Grady and Luanne followed her back to the house. Grady looked back a few times, but Mr. McAfferty never moved. He never said a word. He stayed there for a long time, staring up into the sky.

Grady thought back to that night when Will first came into their lives. He'd seen a shooting star that night, and he'd made a wish on it. He remembered it clearly. His wish was for their family to be back the way they were before Dad died. And now they were.

Their family was whole again.

persnickety-press.com